ISLAND PARTNER

When Giles Patterson deceived her and left her life shattered in pieces, all Sister Helen Meredith wanted was to get away—back to the peace and quiet of home, her beloved Isle of Wight and her GP father. But to her dismay, Helen found that everything had changed. For her father had taken a partner, the quietly persistent Dr Stephen Brett—who had plenty of new-broom ideas for the practice that, he made it clear, should not include Helen.

ISLAND PARTNER

Island Partner

by
Laura MacDonald

Magna Large Print Books
Long Preston, North Yorkshire,
England.

British Library Cataloguing in Publication Data.

MacDonald, Laura
    Island partner.

    A catalogue record for this book is
    available from the British Library

    ISBN 0-7505-0574-5

First published in Great Britain by Mills & Boon Ltd., 1990

Copyright © 1990 by Laura MacDonald

Published in Large Print 1993 by arrangement with Harlequin
Enterprises B.V., Switzerland.

Printed and bound in Great Britain by
T.J. Press (Padstow) Ltd., Cornwall, PL28 8RW.

CHAPTER ONE

The first thing Helen Meredith noticed about the man sitting opposite her on the ferry was the fact that he was reading a medical journal. The second thing she noticed was his hands. Well-shaped and strong-looking, they could easily belong to a doctor...or a surgeon.

Even as the thought crossed her mind she dismissed it. She needed no reminders, and surely the whole object of this trip was to forget a certain surgeon.

The ferry drew out of Portsmouth Harbour and Helen settled herself down for the forty-minute crossing. It was a wet, squally afternoon in November and a warning had just come over the tannoy system that there was a heavy swell running in the Solent. Helen had been prepared for this, for when she had alighted from the London train at Portsmouth Harbour she had found that the normal passenger ferry had been cancelled owing to the rough weather and the passengers diverted to the larger car-ferry.

One or two of the other passengers, probably visitors, seemed a little nervous, but Helen, who had lived on the Isle of Wight for most of her twenty-five years, had made the crossing so often that she wasn't troubled by the prospect of a little rough weather.

She glanced at the man opposite, but he had carried on reading his journal without even looking up. No doubt he too was an Islander, she thought as she absentmindedly studied his clothes. He was certainly dressed for the outdoor life in a dark waxed jacket, Aran sweater and cords.

After a while Helen stood up and crossed to the buffet-bar, where she bought herself a cup of coffee and a chocolate biscuit, carefully carrying them back to her place. But as she reached her table, the ferry, which by this time was well out of the harbour, suddenly lurched alarmingly, causing her to lose her balance. Her cup wobbled precariously, slopping the coffee into the saucer, then, as she desperately sought to steady herself, the ferry lurched again in the opposite direction and this time the cup tipped right over, showering hot coffee over the man reading the journal.

With a smothered exclamation he flung down his magazine, while Helen gasped with embarrassment.

'Oh, I'm dreadfully sorry!' She tried to retrieve the cup, but the ferry rolled again and she stumbled backwards into her seat, falling in an ungainly heap.

By the time she'd sorted herself out the man had picked up the cup from the floor, set it down on the table and was dabbing at his clothes with a white handkerchief.

Helen fumbled in her handbag and produced a handful of tissues, thrusting them across the table in an attempt to make amends. 'Here, take these,' she said breathlessly.

'No, thank you.' His voice was quiet and he sounded quite calm under the circumstances, but this only added to Helen's confusion.

In dismay she watched as he failed to remove the offending brown splash marks from the cream wool of his sweater. 'I really am most awfully sorry,' she muttered, stuffing the tissues back into her bag.

'Think nothing of it,' he replied, and with a resigned shrug he returned his own handkerchief to his pocket. 'Would you like me to get you another coffee?'

For a brief moment Helen's eyes met his cool hazel stare and to her further discomfort she realised there was a trace of amusement there. He probably thought she was some dizzy blonde who was totally incapable of running her own life. He raised his eyebrows and she realised he was waiting for a reply.

Taking a deep breath but still very much aware of the telltale colour in her cheeks, she said, 'No, thank you. I think I'll forget that idea.'

'As you wish.' He strugged again, then picked up his journal and within seconds seemed deeply engrossed.

Helen sat back in her seat, already regretting her refusal of his offer. She really was thirsty, as there had been no buffet car on the London train. She knew she couldn't, however, go and get another drink, for then he really would think her stupid. With a sigh she leaned her head against the seat rest and looked outside at the rolling, foam-capped waves and in the distance the mist-shrouded outline of the Island.

It had been nearly a year since her last

visit home, and whenever she thought about it she felt consumed with guilt. She had of course been in frequent touch with her father either by telephone or letter, but she knew he'd missed her visits. Somehow there just hadn't been the time. Her job as a junior sister on a busy surgical unit at St Luke's Hospital was very demanding, but deep down Helen knew that the real reason for her absence had been her relationship with Giles Patterson. For the past year he had taken up every free moment of her life, and now it was over, and she had automatically found herself wanting to return to her home and things familiar.

Later, as the ferry drew closer to the shoreline of the Island, a quick glance round showed Helen that several of her fellow passengers were already moving towards the exits, some to collect their cars, others to disembark on foot.

She glanced surreptitiously at her silent companion, wondering if he was about to move. She certainly didn't relish the thought of passing him. It would be just her luck for the ferry to lurch again, and this time it would probably be she who would land in his lap. He was still engrossed in his journal, however, and

Helen found herself studying him more closely.

His fair hair, flecked with gold, was thick and wavy, and one lock dropped forward over his left eyebrow. His nose was straight while his mouth, above a firm jawline and slightly cleft chin, was well shaped and full. His eyes, she remembered from when he had looked at her with such cool amusement, were hazel. She judged him to be somewhere in his early thirties.

As if he sensed her scrutiny he suddenly looked up, glanced round at the other passengers, then through the window at the quayside before standing up. With a curt nod in her direction he was gone, disappearing down the gangway to the car deck.

Helen followed more slowly, and as she stepped on to Island soil, her only regret was that she hadn't let anyone know she was coming. If she had, her father's Land Rover would certainly have been in the line of cars at the terminal with the kindly familiar figure at the wheel. She was about to join the passengers for the bus when she saw a solitary taxi. The driver was staring in her direction and she walked towards him, hardly able to believe her luck.

14

'Where to, miss?' The driver's broad Island accent came as a comfort to Helen, who had become accustomed to a Cockney twang or the cultured Oxford tones of Giles Patterson. As the driver opened the boot for her bags, she shivered slightly. She mustn't think of Giles now.

'Dyer's Mead, please,' she said. As he opened the door for her, a dark-coloured hatchback passed them, its tyres making a swishing sound on the tarmac. At the wheel she caught a brief glimpse of the man whom she had drenched with her coffee, then he was gone, swallowed up in the damp November dusk.

Helen slid into the back seat and loosening the belt of her raincoat flicked back her shoulder-length blonde hair, and as the taxi drew out of the terminal she stared out of the window at the darkening afternoon. It was only four o'clock, but already lights were shining in the windows of the houses they passed as they approached the main road.

Had it been a mistake to come home? Helen wondered. It wouldn't be fair to burden her father with her problems, she knew that, for from what Mrs Parkes had implied in her last letter it sounded as if

15

he had troubles of his own. Maybe she needn't tell him too much, perhaps she could just give herself a couple of weeks to recover and decide what she was going to do. All she really needed, she thought with a grimace, was some TLC—tender loving care. How often had she seen that prescribed at St Luke's? Now she was in need of that self-same treatment, not for any physical disability but to heal her wounded pride—and yes, she had to admit it, a broken heart.

She blinked, then realised with a jolt that the taxi driver was speaking to her.

'On holiday, are you, miss?' he asked amiably. 'Weather not been up to much lately. Not for holidays, that is.'

'Oh, I'm not really on holiday,' she leaned forward so that he could hear her above the sound of the engine 'I'm going home.'

'Is that a fact? You live in Dyer's Mead, then?' Curiously he looked at her in the driving mirror. 'My auntie lives there, her name's Lily Prescott—you know her?'

'Why, yes,' she smiled faintly. 'I know Mrs Prescott, she works in the Post Office.'

'Can't say I've seen you before, miss.'

'I've been away for a long time—nursing,

in London.' Silence greeted her statement and she realised he was waiting for further explanation. 'I live at High Pines; my father's Dr Meredith.'

'Ah, is he, now? Well, that explains it.' He sounded satisfied as if he'd solved a mystery. 'Dr Meredith's a good sort, so I've heard.'

The mention of her father's name conjured up a picture of the comfortable old family home where she had grown up, and suddenly, Helen knew she had been right to come. If she couldn't return home in times of trouble, where else was there? Her spirits lifted as she thought of her bedroom overlooking the orchard that Mrs Parkes always kept ready just in case she came home. She was left in no doubt as to the warmth of her welcome, not only from her father and the housekeeper but from the dogs, whose greeting would be little short of ecstatic. With a little sigh she sat back as familiar landmarks flashed past.

The village of Dyer's Mead was situated in the very heart of the Island, tucked away in a fold, a valley beneath the ridge of chalk downs. With dusk rapidly approaching they passed the church, then the village green with its cluster of shops and cottages and on through the village to the very end. Only then did the driver slow down to turn in to a drive flanked by laurel hedges and banks of shiny-leafed rhododendrons.

After Helen had paid the driver she watched him drive away, then, turning, she gazed up at the house. It was built of grey stone, Georgian in style, its proportions neat and symmetrical with three windows on the first floor above two more identical ones which flanked the porch. It all looked so achingly familiar that Helen felt a lump rise to her throat.

In the porch beside the mudscraper stood her father's gumboots, and she smiled as she fitted her key in the lock and, turning the door handle, opened the heavy oak door and stepped into the hall. It was empty and silent, filled only with the smell of lavender furniture polish.

'Hello?' Helen set her bags down on the faded Axminster, then, slipping off her raincoat, she hung it on the stand behind the door. There was no response to her call and she looked down the hall towards the kitchen where she guessed Mrs Parkes was preparing dinner and hadn't heard her come in. She was surprised, however, that the dogs hadn't heard her. It was rare for anyone to enter High Pines unnoticed.

The door to the patients' waiting-room was tightly closed, but her father's consulting-room door stood open and, crossing the hall, Helen looked inside.

The room, with its high sash windows, glass bookcases and large mahogany desk, looked exactly as it had always done. In fact, she thought as her gaze travelled round, taking in the leather couch with its angle-poise lamp, the hand basin and instrument trolley and finally coming to rest on the battered Gladstone bag that her father still insisted on using, some things never changed; no matter what blows life had in store, some things stayed comfortingly the same.

A large framed photograph of herself stood on her father's desk, and with a smile she crossed the room and picked it up. As she stared down at it she ruefully noted how she'd changed in the year or so since it had been taken. The same dark-fringed grey eyes stared back at her, but her face had now lost its rounded look. She knew she had lost weight recently and that hollows had appeared beneath her cheekbones, but, she thought with a sigh, no matter what happened, nothing ever seemed to change the size of her mouth, which she had always considered to be too large.

Leaving the surgery, she made her way to the rear of the large house and the kitchen, and as she pushed open the door the delicious aroma of one of Mrs Parkes' casseroles wafted out to greet her. The kitchen, however, was as deserted as the rest of the house. A quick look into saucepans on the cooker revealed vegetables waiting to be cooked for dinner.

After only a moment's hesitation Helen decided to go up to her room.

With a vague sense of disappointment she walked slowly back into the hall, but as she headed towards the stairs the front doorbell suddenly rang, its urgency shattering the silence.

Putting her bags down again, Helen opened the door.

A woman stood in the porch, a bloodstained piece of material wrapped around her hand. She appeared to be about thirty and had wispy carrot-coloured hair untidily secured with two hairgrips.

'I'm sorry,' she faltered. 'I know I'm too early for surgery, but I've cut my finger. It won't stop bleeding.' There was anxiety in her voice and pain flickered in her pale eyes as she spoke. 'Is the doctor in?' she added when Helen didn't immediately reply.

'Well, it's a bit difficult...you see...' Helen hesitated and glanced back into the silent house.

'It's just the bleeding...I couldn't stop it, and I feel sort of peculiar...'

Helen, her professional instinct taking over, came to a rapid decision. 'You'd better come in.' Her tone was brisk but not unkind. It wouldn't be the first time she'd treated a patient for her father. Several times since she'd qualified, she had assisted with dressings or other minor treatments, usually to hurry things up so that she and her father could spend some time sailing together or walking the downs with the dogs. 'Come in here.' She opened the surgery door and stood back for the woman to enter. 'Now, let's have a look.'

The woman unwrapped her hand and Helen could see the blood seeping from a cut and trickling down her index finger. She indicated for the woman to sit down and instructed her to rest her elbow on a small table to keep her hand upright. 'Now hold the pad tightly round your finger again, while I wash my hands.' She crossed to the sink and as she rinsed the lather from her hands she glanced back at the woman. 'How did you do it?' she asked.

'On a corned beef tin,' she replied. 'I was making my husband's sandwiches for his night shift,' she added, then frowned. 'I don't remember seeing you here before.'

Helen turned again and seeing the woman's anxious expression, she smiled. 'It's all right, I'm Dr Meredith's daughter and I'm a nurse—now tell me, do you still feel faint?'

The woman shook her head. 'No, it's better now I'm sitting down. I never have been one for the sight of blood, it fair turns my stomach.'

Helen took a kidney-shaped dish from one of the cabinets, filled it with water, then added a few drops of antiseptic solution. Carrying it to the table, she set it down, then proceeded to examine the cut. The quantity of blood made it appear far worse than it was, and after Helen had cleansed it with gauze swabs she again applied a pressure pad to staunch the flow of blood.

'Will I need stitches?' The woman looked anxious again.

Helen shook her head. 'No, it looks far worse than it is, but the bleeding is easing up now because you're holding your hand upright. We can repair the damage with some steri-strips, and I can assure you, they won't hurt a bit.'

'Thank goodness for that! I really thought I'd have to have stitches. I was dreading it!'

'It wouldn't have been so bad, you know,' said Helen as she expertly applied the steri-strips to hold the cut together. 'I'd have given you a local anaesthetic to deaden the pain.' As she was speaking, she applied a dry dressing, then slipped a tubular bandage over the injured finger. 'Now, I want you to keep that dry, and you'll need to come back to surgery in about three days to have it checked and the dressing changed.'

'Thank you, Nurse. Thank you very much.' The woman stood up.

'Just a minute,' said Helen, who by this time was once again washing her hands after disposing of the soiled swabs and packaging. 'Is your anti-tetanus up to date?'

The woman looked blank.

'When did you last have a tetanus injection?' said Helen patiently.

'I don't know. Oh, wait a minute—yes, I do. It was when that dog bit me—must have been five years ago. I remember because it was on our Scott's fifth birthday, and he's ten now.'

'In that case you'll only need a booster,' said Helen, drying her hands on a paper towel. 'If you'll just slip off your coat I'll fetch your records from the office. Oh, it might be a help if I knew your name.' She paused in the doorway and smiled.

'It's Arnold—Maureen Arnold.'

'And what's your address?'

'Twenty-six, Sorrell Close.'

'Sorrell Close? Where's that?'

Maureen Arnold looked up in surprise, 'Up on the new estate.' With her good hand she waved vaguely behind her.

'I see—you'll have to excuse my ignorance, I've been away from Dyer's Mead for a while,' Helen explained.

'Have you?' Maureen Arnold stared at her with renewed interest. 'Well, you'll see a few changes, then, and that's a fact.'

In the room that her father used as an office were several large filing cabinets, and Helen opened the first one and quickly flicked through the 'A's, but there was no sign of Maureen Arnold's records. She collected a tetanus report form, then opened the fridge in the corner of the room and took an injection ampoule from its box.

'Your records appear to be out for some reason, Mrs Arnold,' she said as she returned to the surgery. 'Perhaps you've visited the doctor recently?'

The woman frowned. 'No, I haven't, although I was supposed to.' She coloured slightly. 'I had a letter about one of those smear tests, but I haven't been for one yet. I don't fancy it somehow. It's embarrassing with a man doctor.'

'You really should, Mrs Arnold,' said Helen as she drew up the injection, administering it before the woman had time to realise what she was doing. 'Smear tests are extremely important. Right, that's done.' She dabbed Maureen Arnold's arm. 'You may put your coat on again. Now, why don't you mention your smear to the doctor when you come back to have your dressing checked?'

'Oh, I couldn't do that, I'd have to make an appointment.'

'But Dr Meredith doesn't have an appointment system,' said Helen, then added, 'At least, he didn't the last time I was here, but maybe that's one of the changes you were talking about.' She laughed.

'Dr Meredith's not my doctor.'

Helen had begun to fill in the anti-tetanus report form, but she stopped and stared at the woman, her pen poised in the air. 'But I thought you said you lived here in Dyer's Mead...I assumed...'

'I do live here, but it's the other doctor I see. He's very nice, but he's so young, and that's why I was embarrassed about—' She broke off, startled, as the surgery door suddenly opened. 'Oh, hello, Dr Brett,' she said, a blush covering her freckled face again. 'We were just talking about you.'

Helen spun round. The man was very tall, his broad-shouldered frame almost filling the doorway, a lock of hair fell over one eyebrow, and to Helen's dismay, for the second time that day she found herself staring into a pair of cool hazel eyes.

CHAPTER TWO

Helen stared at him in dismay. What in the world was he, of all people, doing in her father's surgery? Then in a flash, as she stared from him to Maureen Arnold, she understood. Mrs Arnold had called him 'Doctor', confirming Helen's own earlier suspicions, so the only explanation was that he was a locum covering for her father for some reason.

His eyes had narrowed suspiciously as he took in the situation, then in a quiet deep voice that Helen had already heard, he said, 'Would someone mind telling me what's going on?'

As Helen hesitated, trying to find the right words, Maureen Arnold intervened. 'It's all my fault, Dr Brett. I'd cut my hand, you see, on a corned beef tin, and this lady has kindly bound it up for me.'

'Has she indeed?' He raised his eyebrows and looked at Helen is surprise. 'Well, I'm sure that's very commendable of her, but think I'd better take a look, don't you?'

He moved towards Maureen Arnold, and Helen stiffened. How dared he check her work! Before he had a chance to remove the tubular bandage, she said, 'I don't think you'll find it necessary to do that—I'm a nursing sister and I've treated the cut in the usual way with steri-strips and a dry dressing.' It was a direct challenge and for a moment she had the satisfaction of seeing him hesitate, then to her annoyance he gave a slight shrug and made as if to continue what he was doing. This time it was Maureen Arnold who offered a further explanation.

'I'm sure it's quite all right, Doctor.' She gave a nervous laugh. 'I was a bit worried who this lady was as well, seeing I've never seen her here before, then, when she said she was a nurse and Dr Meredith's daughter, I thought it must be all right.' In the silence which followed, Maureen looked anxiously from Helen to Dr Brett.

Helen found herself holding her breath as she watched him. Would he let the woman's explanation suffice now that he knew who she was or would he still insist on checking her work?

Slowly he let go of the patient's bandaged hand and stepped back, then glancing at the table, he said calmly, 'I see Sister has given you a tetanus booster, Mrs Arnold. Good. Look after that cut, keep the dressing dry and I'll see you in surgery in a few days.' He walked her to the door, then as Helen heard the front door close he came back into the room.

His face was expressionless, but Helen sensed he was annoyed. She took a deep breath. 'I apologise if you think I may have acted out of turn,' she said quickly, not giving him a chance to level any accusations. 'But I can assure you my father won't have any objections. I've assisted him many times in the past and I know he won't mind, especially as it was an emergency and there was no one else here.'

'I was here.' His reply was pointed and only endorsed Helen's earlier feeling that he was annoyed. She bit her lip, but before she had time to say anything further, he held out his hand and said, 'We don't seem to have got off to a very good start, do we? Maybe we should go back to the beginning and try again. I'm Stephen Brett.'

She only hesitated for a fraction of a second before stepping forward and putting her hand in his. His fingers gripped hers in a strong clasp. 'Helen Meredith,' she replied with a brief nod.

An awkward little silence followed, during which Stephen Brett glanced again at the table, the form and empty ampoule. 'I'd better enter this in the patient's notes,' he said.

'I would have done that,' Helen explained hurriedly, 'but her notes weren't in the files.' She nodded towards the office as she spoke.

He stared at her for a moment. 'Her notes wouldn't be in there.'

'Why?' She looked puzzled.

'Because Maureen Arnold is my patient, not Dr Meredith's.'

Helen frowned. 'She said something to that effect, but I thought she must have made a mistake.'

'Why should you think that?'

'Well, patients don't usually register with a locum, do they?'

He didn't answer immediately, and as she stared at him the germ of an awful possibility began to form in the back of her mind. She took a deep breath. 'You are a locum—aren't you?'

The faintly annoyed air that she had detected earlier had gone, replaced now by an almost infuriating look of amusement.

'No, I'm not a locum,' he replied patiently, 'I'm your father's new partner.'

Helen stared at him with a mixture of dismay and astonishment. No wonder he'd been annoyed to find her treating one of his patients! Desperately she tried to cover her embarrassment, then, as the full implication of what he had just said finally hit her, she looked up at him and frowned.

'I don't understand. Why has my father taken a partner?' It was the one thing Oliver Meredith had vowed never to do, determined as he was to keep the practice single-handed until he retired in a couple of years' time.

'Your father hadn't told you?' He looked curious.

Helen shook her head, suddenly feeling foolish in front of this stranger who must wonder whatever sort of relationship she had with her father if she didn't know such basic facts.

'I believe he was pushed to it by sheer pressure of work—his list had grown out of all proportion. But I think you'd better ask him for yourself.' As he was speaking they heard the front door open and a split

31

second later they were almost bowled over by a large, damp, over-enthusiastic springer spaniel who charged into the surgery, shook himself, then made a beeline for Stephen Brett.

He bent down to pat the dog while Helen said, 'Hello, Plummer, old boy.'

The dog hesitated, then crossed the room for its welcome from Helen before returning almost immediately to the new doctor.

She had time for only a momentary stab of disappointment before she heard her father's voice from the hall.

'Is that you, Stephen?' he called. 'How was your trip? I say, whose bags are these—I almost tripped over them...'

Neither of them moved, then Oliver Meredith appeared in the doorway, grumbling to himself. As he caught sight of Helen he stopped dead, staring at her in astonishment, while Helen felt a stab of dismay when she saw how tired and old he was looking.

'Helen, my dear child! Whatever are you doing here?' He stared from her to Stephen Brett in disbelief.

'I found her treating one of my patients.' Dr Brett raised one eyebrow.

Helen stepped forward into her father's welcoming embrace just as another dog suddenly appeared. This time it was an elderly black Labrador who thumped his tail ecstatically at the sight of her.

Drawing away from her father, she leaned down and patted the old dog. 'At least you're pleased to see me, aren't you, Jason? It's more than Plummer was.' She pulled a face.

'I'm afraid you'll find Plummer has been very fickle and transferred his affections,' said Oliver Meredith with a wry glance at the younger man.

'I rather gathered that,' replied Helen.

There was an awkward silence, then her father cleared his throat. 'But enough of dogs—you haven't answered my question. What are you doing here?'

'It's a long story.' Helen was suddenly very conscious of Stephen Brett's eyes upon her, and she certainly didn't intend to embark on any explanations in front of him.

'But why didn't you let us know you were coming? I'd have come to meet you. However did you get here from the ferry?'

'By taxi,' replied Helen shortly, unable

to resist a glance at Stephen Brett, who for a fraction of a second looked uncomfortable.

Oliver must have intercepted the glance, for he quickly asked, 'I say, have you two introduced yourselves?'

'Actually we met on the ferry.' Helen couldn't resist allowing a tinge of sarcasm to enter her tone. It would do him good to feel uncomfortable.

'Really?' Oliver looked surprised.

'Yes,' Stephen Brett's reply was cool. 'Of course, I had no idea then that this lady was your daughter. Besides, I was too busy at the time mopping up her coffee which had landed in my lap.'

For a moment Oliver's expression was almost comical, while Helen's gaze flew to Stephen Brett's cream sweater where sure enough the offending stains could be seen.

The younger man allowed himself a smile. 'I shouldn't think it was deliberate,' he said, glancing at Helen, who found herself blushing under that cool, faintly amused gaze. 'It was a very rough crossing.'

'Oh, I see, one of those,' Helen's father smiled knowingly. Then he turned once again to his daughter. 'Helen, it really is wonderful to see you. How long are you able to stay?'

She hesitated and looked keenly at her father. Ever since he had appeared she had been struck by the change in him. He had aged since the last time she had been home. His grey hair had receded and in places appeared almost white, while the lines on his face, especially those between nose and mouth, were deeply defined. His blue eyes, however, had the same twinkle about them that she remembered so well. As she finished her brief scrutiny of his features she realised he was still waiting for some sort of explanation for her sudden arrival. 'I'm not really sure at the moment just how long I'll be here.'

Her father's eyes narrowed. 'Is Giles with you?'

Helen shook her head, but before she lowered her gaze, she noticed a flicker of interest in Stephen Brett's eyes. 'No,' she said shortly, 'Giles isn't with me.'

There was another awkward pause, then her father said briskly, 'I see. Well, we'll chat later, shall we?'

'Yes, I imagine we have several things to discuss,' Helen replied, allowing her gaze to flicker imperceptibly to the young doctor.

'Yes, quite. Now tell me,' Oliver, evidently sensing the tension, skilfully changed the subject, 'have you seen Mrs Parkes yet? You must be famished and it is, I believe, time for tea.' He glanced at his watch.

'Mrs Parkes wasn't in the kitchen when I arrived,' Helen replied, wishing that this meeting between herself and her father could have been in private.

'Of course, it's her WI meeting this afternoon, but she should be back soon.'

'In that case I'll pop upstairs and freshen up,' said Helen. Not giving either man a chance to say anything further, she hurried from the surgery, through the hall and up the stairs.

She was glad to escape from the cool stare of Dr Stephen Brett—she couldn't imagine what had prompted her father to take a partner when he had always been so much against it—but she certainly meant to find out.

She paused for a moment on the landing looking round at the bedroom doors, then, stepping forward, she opened the door of the room that had been hers since childhood, the room that Mrs Parkes kept ready and aired just in case she was able to spend some time at home.

Then in the open doorway she stopped. Her usual patterned curtains had been replaced by a pair in heavy blue velour, and a glance at the bed revealed a royal blue candlewick bedspread instead of her duvet with its country flower design. Wildly she looked around. On the dressing-table were a set of hairbrushes and a black leather travelling case, while on the bedside cabinet there stood an unfamiliar clock radio.

Angrily Helen crossed the room, tugged open the oak wardrobe and stared at the neat row of men's clothing and the shoes on the floor. With an exclamation she pushed the wardrobe door shut, then a slight sound behind her made her spin round. Once again Stephen Brett had quietly caught her unawares, for she hadn't realised he would actually be living in the house. At last, in spite of her growing sense of irritation, she was forced to mutter and apology, for he was, after all, a guest in her father's house.

He, however, barred her way as she attempted to pass him in the doorway, compelling her to look up at him. 'It seems,' he said quietly, 'that I should be the one to apologise. I didn't know this was your bedroom.'

Helen shrugged, trying to give the impression that she couldn't care less. 'I'm hardly ever at home these days—I just assumed too much, that's all. I'll be perfectly all right in the guest-room.'

He shook his head. 'On the contrary, that's where I should be.' His reply was curt, then he added, 'I'll move my gear out—give me half an hour.'

'Certainly not!' Helen's tone was suddenly crisp, then in the awkward pause that followed there came the sound of someone calling her name from the hall below.

'Ah, there's Mrs Parkes,' Helen said in relief, attempting to pass him again, but still he stood in her way, the expression in his hazel eyes unreadable as he looked down into hers.

In spite of her annoyance at this man's presence in her home she felt a tingle run the length of her spine. There was an unusual attractiveness about him, and she had the sudden feeling that there was more to Dr Stephen Brett than she had at first realised. As Mrs Parkes called out again she took a deep breath and said,

'Excuse me, please.'

At last he stood aside, but still left very little room for her to pass, and as she squeezed by, her shoulder brushed against his chest and momentarily she caught the scent of his aftershave, a tangy, outdoor scent very different from the deep musky one that Giles used. With her head down Helen hurried across the landing. So far her home coming left much to be desired, for apart from her father's obvious pleasure at her sudden arrival, very little else had been as she had anticipated. Even Plummer's welcome had been less than enthusiastic. But already she knew that the real reason for her sense of unease was the man who stood silently on the landing watching her descend the stairs.

The embarrassing incident on the ferry would have been bad enough in itself, but on top of that the self-same man seemed to be firmly ensconced not only in her family home but in her own bedroom, the room she had always considered as her retreat from the world.

The greeting Helen received from Mrs Parkes did something to make up for her previous disappointments, and she followed the plump, motherly figure into the kitchen, where she watched her hang up her coat, tie on her pinafore and fill the kettle.

Mrs Parkes had been the housekeeper at High Pines for as long as Helen could remember. When Helen's mother, Patricia, had been alive, Mrs Parkes had come on a daily basis to help with the cleaning. When Mrs Meredith had died ten years previously, Mrs Parkes had moved in on a permanent basis to look after the doctor and his fifteen-year-old daughter.

'You should have let us know you were coming, dear,' said Mrs Parkes, shooing Plummer out of her way.

Helen sighed. 'Yes, I'm beginning to think I should, but it's never mattered before.'

Mrs Parkes spooned tea into a large brown teapot, then paused and looked at Helen, her kindly face anxious. 'I'm sorry about your room, love, but it seemed only right to give the best room to Dr Brett—it's only until he finds a place of his own, and it has been such a long time since you were last here...you don't mind, do you?'

She looked so worried that Helen forced a reassuring smile. 'Of course not, Parky, you did the right thing. But,' she glanced over her shoulder as if expecting to find that Dr Brett had crept up on her again, 'what I don't understand is, what's he doing here? I haven't had a chance to ask Dad yet.'

'Well, you know I wrote and told you how busy your dad had been?'

Helen nodded, and felt a sudden twinge of guilt. She remembered receiving the letter, and thinking that she should pay a visit to her father, but then she had become so wrapped up in her own problems that she'd let the matter slide.

'He'd got really run down,' Mrs Parkes went on as she brewed the tea. 'He wasn't himself at all, then last summer that caravan park opened at the end of the village and it was one batch of visitors after another. Ringing the doorbell, they were all times of the day and night. You wouldn't believe some of the things they came for! Anyway, your poor father began to look quite ill—he doesn't look right now...'

'I noticed,' said Helen quietly. 'Sorry, Parky, go on. What happened?'

'Well, I told him it was time he had some help. But would he listen? You know how stubborn he is and how he's always said that he'd keep this a one-man practice.' As she spoke Mrs Parkes set out cups on a tray.

'So what made him change his mind?' asked Helen curiously. 'At first I thought this Dr Brett might simply be a locum helping out for a few days as we've had in the past, but he said he was a partner.' Suddenly she felt she wanted to hear Mrs Parkes' version of what had prompted this drastic move before she heard her father's. She knew he would make light of whatever the circumstances had been.

'It was what's happening up in Skinner's Fields,' said Mrs Parkes darkly. 'That's what finally did it.'

'Whatever do you mean?' Helen looked startled as all sorts of unlikely images flitted through her brain.

'It was that new estate that they're building up there.' There was no disguising the disgust in her voice. 'We all fought it—got up a petition, even had one of those MPs down here—but they won in the end. They started building houses and before we knew where we were people were moving in. Goodness knows where they've all come from. Mainlanders, most of them.' She sniffed. 'But that's what did it for your father. They've been turning up in droves to register with him, poor man.' Deftly she poured the tea for Helen and herself, then set a smaller pot on the tray for the doctors.

'So what happened?' asked Helen, beginning now to understand the reason for the father's appearance.

'Well, just when I thought he'd crack under the strain of it all, he had a visit from one of those high-up ones in that Committee—you know the one I mean.'

Helen nodded. 'The Family Practitioner Committee. Yes, I know.'

'Your father was pretty quiet for a couple of days after that, then one morning after surgery, he called me in and introduced me to Dr Brett. He told me afterwards that the extra work had forced him to take a partner and that Dr Brett would be staying with us until he could get fixed up with a place of his own.'

'But why didn't he tell me?' Helen bit her lip. 'He never mentioned any of this in his letters or on the phone.'

'He said you weren't to be worried and that he wanted to tell you himself when you came home for Christmas. There wasn't much I could do, was there, dear?'

She looked so anxious that Helen forced

another smile. 'No, I suppose not. But I wish I'd known things were so hectic, I'd have come sooner...'

By this time Mrs Parkes had picked up the tray and started towards the door, but she paused then and half turned towards Helen. 'Is Mr Patterson with you, dear?'

'No, Parky,' Helen replied quietly. 'I'm alone.'

'I see.' The housekeeper hesitated a moment longer, then said, 'I'll just take this through for the doctors, it's nearly time for evening surgery. I won't be long.'

As she waited, Helen sipped her tea and glanced round at the familiar kitchen full of objects that reminded her of her childhood. She felt shaken by what Mrs Parkes had just told her, for she knew that her father must indeed have reached the end of his tether to have taken the drastic measures he had. If only she'd visited a little more often she would have been more aware of that had been happening. As it was, she'd been so involved with her own life and her affair with Giles Patterson that she'd been oblivious to anything else. She shifted in her chair. Even the thought of him still brought her pain, and as Mrs Parkes bustled back into the kitchen she stood up abruptly, draining her cup. She wasn't ready to discuss Giles yet, so to avert any further questions she carried her cup and saucer to the sink and asked casually, 'So how's it working out, Parky? Between the two doctors? I just can't imagine Dad with a partner.'

Mrs Parkes smiled, then pushing the kitchen door to behind her, she leaned towards her. 'Oh, they've had their clashes already. Dr Brett's very quiet, but he can be stubborn.'

'I can't imagine my father giving in too often,' Helen remarked wryly. 'He's had things his own way too long.'

'You're right, but from what I've heard, Dr Brett wants to make changes. He's got lots of modern ideas, but your father says he's quite happy with the way things are. Like I say, there's been a few ding-dongs in the last few weeks and I shouldn't be surprised if there aren't a few more. Mind you, I have to say, in spite of my loyalty to your father—and no one could question that—I do like young Dr Brett. He may be quiet—shy, some would say—but he has charm, he's a gentleman, and that's something you don't very often find these days. Now that's enough of my gossiping,' she glanced at the large kitchen clock, 'I must get this apple crumble in the oven.'

'Apple crumble? Oh, Parky, my favourite!' Helen laughed. 'There, you must have known I was coming.'

'Oh, yes, dear, it was your favourite, wasn't it? But do you know what? It also happens to be Dr Brett's favourite,' Mrs Parkes straightened up from the cooker, 'I made it especially for him because he enjoyed it so much the last time. Now, I think we'd better go upstairs and sort out the spare room for you.'

Slowly Helen followed Mrs Parkes from the kitchen. Suddenly her appetite for apple crumble seemed to have vanished.

CHAPTER THREE

In the hall Helen found that her bags had disappeared. No doubt her father had carried them upstairs, she thought, then wondered fleetingly whether it could have been Stephen Brett who had done so. Even as the thought crossed her mind she glanced into the waiting-room where several patients were already waiting for evening surgery to begin. At that moment Stephen Brett appeared through a doorway on the far side of the room and called the first patient. An elderly man folded his newspaper and stood up, and in that instant Helen's eyes met those of Dr Brett across the room. Quickly she averted her gaze and followed Mrs Parkes up the stairs.

Once they were out of earshot Helen said, 'Parky, where does Dr Brett hold his surgery?'

Mrs Parkes paused before opening the door of the spare bedroom and turned to her. 'We cleared out the snug for him—it's just about the right size.'

For the umpteenth time that day Helen felt a stab of dismay. The snug, to her, meant just what it implied, a room bright with sunshine on a summer's morning or a welcome corner on cold afternoons with a cheerful log fire burning in the grate. It was a room where on countless occasions she had sought refuge and curled up for hours with a good book. Now, it seemed, it was his, an antiseptic-smelling, clinical room stripped of its comfort and charm.

The guest bedroom, however, wasn't as

austere as she remembered it, and within half an hour she and Mrs Parkes had it looking fresh and comfortable with crisp clean sheets, bowls of pot-pourri on the dressing-table and her personal possessions unpacked.

Helen was still finding it difficult to accept the idea of her father's having a partner and one who seemed to have made himself so very much at home. As she dressed for dinner she found her thoughts wandering to the man who seemed to have made such an impression on Mrs Parkes, and on his patients, if Maureen Arnold was anything to go by, for the look she had given him as she had left the surgery had been little short of naked admiration.

The man obviously had charm, as Mrs Parkes had observed, even if it was in an understated sort of way, but Helen was in no frame of mind to succumb to any man's charm.

The recent events in her life had left her feeling battered and very vulnerable, and the way she was feeling she doubted she would ever find anyone she could love as she had loved Giles Patterson. As she secured her hair with two ceramic slides it crossed her mind that Stephen Brett was the exact opposite to Giles. He was quiet, reserved and obviously the outdoor, country type, whereas Giles had been an extrovert, smooth and sophisticated.

Sudden angry tears sprang to her eyes as she thought of Giles, and helplessly she stared at her reflection in the mirror. Oh, why had she loved him so much? Would she ever get over him? But she had to, she knew that.

Resolutely she stood up, blinking back her tears. She'd burnt her boats now and there was no going back. Taking a deep breath, she smoothed down the skirt of the blue jersey dress she'd chosen to wear, then with her head high she made her way downstairs to the sitting-room where her father was waiting for her. She was relieved to see he was alone.

His tired face lit up as she came into the room. 'Helen, my dear. May I get you a drink?'

She smiled and took a seat near the fire. 'Yes, please,' she said, leaning her head against the back of the deep, comfortable sofa. Plummer looked up from the hearthrug, then stood up, stretched and padded over to Helen where he rested his head on her lap and stared beseechingly up into her face.

'So you've come to make amends, have you?' Helen fondled his head and long ears, and he sighed blissfully.

'It really is good to have you home, Helen.' Her father handed her a glass of sherry and, as her fingers closed round the stem of the glass, the cut crystal flashed in the light from the fire.

As she sipped her drink and felt the tensions of the past few hours slip away she watched her father, who stood before the fire, his glass of whisky and soda in his hand. 'It seems to me it's a good thing I have come home,' she replied, 'If I hadn't, I wonder how long it would have been before I was told what's been going on.'

Her father looked uncomfortable and lowered his gaze. 'I'm sure I don't know what you're talking about,' he muttered into his glass.

'And I'm sure you do. Why didn't you tell me?' she demanded. 'The last thing in the world I would have expected you to do would have been to take a partner.'

He shrugged, unable to meet her eyes. 'Ah, well, needs must, you know...and then I had old Robinson down here from the

FPC haranguing me about my workload.'

'That's not what I'm talking about,' Helen interrupted crisply.

'Then what...?'

'I just feel it would have been nice to have been told what was happening instead of finding a strange man installed in my bedroom.'

Oliver Meredith sighed deeply, then allowed himself a rueful smile. 'I stand corrected, and I apologise.'

Helen was forced to smile at his contrite expression. 'Accepted. But as a matter of interest, why didn't you tell me?'

He paused, sipping his whisky thoughtfully, then he said, 'For a start, I didn't want you to worry, as I knew you would when you heard I'd taken a partner, and secondly, I didn't feel it was the sort of thing I wanted to explain in a letter.'

'So when was I to find out?' She raised her eyebrows enquiringly.

'I was waiting until Christmas, until you came down with Giles. But now you're here...It really is a wonderful surprise, Helen.'

'I don't know how long I shall be here,' Helen said after a moment's silence.

'Don't worry. I know your time is

precious.' Her father smiled at her over the rim of his glass. 'I'm just grateful for whatever time you can spare.'

She swallowed and set her glass down carefully on a small leather-topped coffee table. 'You don't understand. When I said I didn't know how long I should be here, I meant that it may be for rather longer than you thought.'

Oliver Meredith raised his eyebrows in surprise. 'But that's even better. You know you can always stay as long as you like. After all, this is your home...but,' his eyes narrowed, 'what about your job?'

'I've left St Luke's,' Helen replied quietly, staring into the fire as she spoke.

There was a moment's silence while Oliver digested this piece of information, then he said, 'I don't understand, Helen. St Luke's has always been everything to you. I thought you loved your life there...and surely you were up for regrading?'

'That's right, I was...but I was forced to resign...it was for personal reasons. I'm sorry, Dad, but I'm not sure I'm ready to talk about it yet.' Helen went on stroking Plummer's head, but her hands were shaking.

Her father remained silent for some

moments, then he said, 'It seems, Helen, that I haven't been the only one keeping secrets...' He paused and then asked the inevitable question. 'Does your decision have anything to do with Giles Patterson? Just answer me that for the time being.'

She looked up at him and her eyes glistened in the firelight. 'Yes, Dad.' she whispered. 'It has everything to do with him—we're finished...' Her voice quavered and she trailed off.

He waited a moment before continuing, then when he spoke his tone was gentle. 'I'm sorry, my dear. Very sorry.'

Helen shrugged slightly. 'I'm not certain yet what I want to do, although it did cross my mind that I might see if they have any vacancies at the hospital in Newport, preferably on the surgical unit.'

'They may well have—we'll talk about it later...Ah, here's Stephen.' They both looked up as Stephen Brett came into the room. 'Come and join us for a drink,' said Oliver.

He had changed from his jumper and cords into casual grey trousers, a polo-necked sweater and a navy blue jacket, and after only a moment's hesitation he joined Helen and her father in front of the fire.

Plummer promptly left Helen and rubbed himself against the newcomer's legs in such a gesture of adoration that even Helen was forced to smile at his fickle behaviour.

'Stephen, what will you have?' asked Oliver, then when the younger man refused, he said, 'Oh, come now, this is a special occasion. I have my daughter home again.' It suddenly became apparent that it was important to the older man that they should get along, and Helen knew she would have to make some sort of effort if she were to reverse the disastrous first impression she must have given. She felt reluctant to do so, for she still thought of the young doctor as an intruder, especially now, when she so desperately wanted the seclusion of her home and the support of her family. However, when he accepted a drink, obviously in her honour, she took a deep breath.

'I believe I owe you an apology, Dr Brett,' she murmured.

He turned to her, raising his eyebrows. 'I wasn't aware that you did—and it's Stephen, by the way.'

'I shouldn't have treated your patient,' said Helen. 'Especially when you were on the premises.'

'I think we can overlook it, Sister Meredith, especially as you were unaware of the situation at the time.' As he spoke she once again detected the glimmer of amusement in his eyes.

'Thank you,' she inclined her head, then added, 'and please call me Helen. As I said at the time, it came as second nature to treat Mrs Arnold's cut, it's the sort of thing I've done so many times before to help out.'

Her father nodded. 'That's quite right. Many's the time Helen's lent a hand when she's been here on holiday.'

'It endorses what I've been saying all along, Oliver,' replied Stephen, taking a sip of his drink. 'This practice really could do with a nurse.'

Oliver gave a short laugh. 'This is all part of Stephen's programme of reformation,' he explained to Helen. 'He seems to think that I've been living in the Dark Ages and need pulling into the twentieth century by my boot straps. He's been all for employing a nurse who will also do reception and administration work.'

'And you disagree?' Helen glanced from one to the other.

'I don't think we warrant it,' Oliver shrugged.

'But you have to admit the paperwork is getting out of control,' remarked Stephen mildly.

'Maybe, maybe not, but you're taking things to extremes with that wretched computer you want to install.'

Stephen smiled, and Oliver turned to Helen in exasperation. 'That's where he's been today, to the mainland to see some computer demonstration of all things. Dare we ask how it went, Stephen?'

'Excellent. In fact I'm more convinced than ever it's just what we need.'

'God help us!' Oliver rolled his eyes in horror, then Mrs Parkes appeared in the doorway to tell them that dinner was ready.

During dinner, time and again Helen found her gaze drawn towards Stephen. There was something about his quiet manner that fascinated her. It was when he leaned forward to cut himself a wedge of cheese from the cheeseboard that she found it difficult to tear her eyes away from his hands. In fact, she remembered, it had been his hands that had been one of the first things she had noticed about him

56

on the ferry when she had rightly assumed that he might be a doctor.

Once again, Helen found herself comparing him to Giles, and once again she was struck by the contrast. Giles was slim, very dark in colouring, slightly built and incredibly handsome, and his hands, although equally strong, were smooth and brown, the fingers as long and beautifully shaped as those of a pianist. With Stephen Brett one could be forgiven for imagining him to be a sportsman from the sheer size of him, his muscular build and healthy outdoor complexion.

It was while they were drinking their coffee that the conversation returned once more to the running of the practice and Stephen asked Oliver if he had reconsidered adopting an appointment system.

'Not really,' replied the older man with a shrug. 'I don't see why we can't continue as we have been. The two systems seem to be running perfectly adequately together, don't they?' When Stephen didn't immediately reply, Oliver threw him a sharp look. 'Well, don't they?' he demanded.

Helen, sensing a rising of tension, looked

quickly at Stephen, who was calmly stirring his coffee.

'Let's just say I've overheard mutterings in the waiting-room,' he replied.

'What do you mean, mutterings?' Oliver, clearly affronted, glared at the younger doctor.

'If you have a group of people booked in on appointments and another group who simply come and wait their turn, then it's inevitable that you'll get resentment from those who feel they're waiting longer than others.'

'Well, I don't have time to make appointments,' Oliver replied tetchily, 'and I don't think it's fair to expect Mrs Parkes to do so either. She has enough to do answering emergency calls without that.'

Helen turned to Stephen in surprise. 'Mrs Parkes makes your appointments?'

'At the moment, yes,' he replied coolly. 'She has my appointment book in the kitchen, but it's something which is not satisfactory and I know it can't continue. It's one of the reasons why I want to employ a practice nurse who will also deal with reception.'

'So we're back to that again,' Oliver

sighed. 'I'm still not convinced. I can't believe there would be enough for a practice nurse to do.'

'I have several other schemes to try out,' said Stephen.

'I'll bet you have,' replied Oliver darkly.

'What sort of schemes did you have in mind?' asked Helen, looking at Stephen.

'Ante-natal and diabetic clinics for a start. A family planning clinic also—I feel that's essential, especially now with the young families we have moving into the area on the new estate.'

'I've always coped perfectly adequately giving that sort of advice during daily surgery,' said Oliver stiffly.

'I'm not disputing that, Oliver, but I feel very strongly that there are times when the presence of a female nurse could be very beneficial. For example, I would dearly love to set up a Well Woman clinic, and for cytology a nurse is essential. What do you think, Helen?'

He took her by surprise asking for her opinion, and, although she didn't wish to appear disloyal to her father, Helen found herself reluctantly agreeing with Stephen. 'I think he could be right, Dad,' she replied slowly, and when her father glared indignantly at her she continued, 'The lady I saw this afternoon, Mrs Arnold—she mentioned that she'd been called for a cervical smear but that she was embarrassed to see a male doctor.'

Oliver was silent for a moment, then he shrugged. 'All right, I take your point, but I'm still uncertain about the workload warranting a full-time nurse.'

'What we really need is for someone to take the job on a temporary basis,' said Stephen, 'just to see how things work out...'

Oliver looked up sharply, then put his cup down into its saucer with a noisy rattle. 'I say, the answer's staring us in the face!' He turned to his daughter. 'Helen, you're looking for a job!'

Helen looked up, startled. 'Yes, but not that, Dad. I'm sorry, but that's not my cup of tea at all.'

'But it would only be temporary, you heard what Stephen said...'

'Maybe so...but I'd miss the wards too much. As I said earlier, I was going to see if they had a job up at the hospital.'

'They may not have a vacancy for a

sister at the moment, and you don't want down-grading, do you? Go on, Helen, give it a try.'

Helen hesitated, looking from one to the other. Her father had an eager expression on on his face, but Stephen had his head down.

'Well, maybe I'll think about it, but it would be strictly on the understanding that it would only be temporary.'

'Of course, Helen, you have your career to think of. You've worked too hard to lose that, but it would be marvellous if you could join us for a while. I think I could cope with you setting up Stephen's schemes, but I'm not sure I could take some stiff and starchy stranger. What do you say, Stephen?'

In the silence that followed Oliver's question the faint ringing of the telephone could be heard. Both men from sheer habit lifted their heads and listened, then, when the ringing stopped and both were obviously satisfied that Mrs Parkes had answered it, Oliver turned again to Stephen.

'Well,' he demanded impatiently, 'don't you think it's an excellent idea?'

Helen glanced at Stephen, but still he

hesitated, the slowly he looked up and she found herself once again looking into that cool hazel stare.

'I don't know,' he replied quietly.

'What d'you mean, you don't know?' Oliver was dabbing his mouth with his napkin, but he paused, the napkin still at his lips, and stared incredulously at Stephen. 'It's an excellent idea. What reason could you possibly have for objecting?'

'I don't agree with members of the same family working together. From my experience it very rarely works...' Stephen was interrupted as Mrs Parkes knocked on the door and entered the dining-room.

'I'm sorry, gentlemen,' she said. 'It's an emergency call. Tom Attrill from the farm rang to say that his lad Simon is having difficulty breathing with his asthma.'

'Right, Mrs Parkes, thank you.' Oliver stood up.

'No, Oliver, I'll go. You stay and talk to Helen.' Stephen rose to his feet. 'You must have a lot to catch up on.'

'That's awfully decent of you, old man. But the Attrills are my patients.'

'I know,' smiled Stephen. 'But that is what partnership is all about. Is there anything I need to know?'

'Yes—the lad is on salbutamol, two-milligram tablets and inhalers, and earlier this week I started him on a course of ampicillin.'

'Right, thanks.' Stephen rose to his feet. 'I'll get over there and take a nebuliser with me.' With a brief nod to Helen and Oliver he was gone.

In the silence that followed his departure, Helen toyed with a knife, drawing patterns on the tablecloth, then, glancing at her father, she said, 'That's the first time ever I've known you not to have to go on an emergency.'

Oliver nodded. 'I agree. I suppose having a partner does have its compensations, but,' he stirred uneasily, 'I'm finding it very hard to adapt. I'm too long in the tooth, Helen, to start learning new tricks, and young Brett is too full of ideas for my liking. Mind you,' he suddenly brightened, 'I must say it would be nice having you working with us.'

'Just hold on a minute, Dad!' Helen held up her hand in protest. 'I haven't agreed to anything yet.'

'No, but you did say you'd think about it.'

'That was before your partner showed

his disapproval,' she replied acidly. 'He certainly didn't seem to like the idea of my working here.'

'He can't have it all his own way, for heaven's sake!' Oliver exploded.

He looked so indignant that Helen was forced to smile and found herself half agreeing that it might indeed be interesting to take the job on a month's trial, just to confound the new partner, then thoughtfully she went back to tracing the patterns on the cloth. Somehow she felt she'd got off to a very bad start with Dr Stephen Brett, but maybe it wasn't entirely her fault. Maybe he just didn't like women.

'Is he married?' she asked without looking up.

'Married? Stephen?' Oliver gave a short laugh. 'Not on your life! A confirmed bachelor, that one.' He was silent for a moment, then hesitantly he said, 'While we're on the subject of marriage, Helen, do you feel able to tell me what happened between you and Patterson? I was quite prepared for marriage plans there, you know. What was the problem?'

Helen was silent for a moment battling with her emotions, then quietly she said,

'That was the problem.'

'What?' Oliver looked puzzled.

'Marriage.'

'You mean he didn't want to get married?'

Helen took a deep breath. 'No, Dad, he already was married.'

CHAPTER FOUR

'He was what?' Oliver stared aghast at Helen.

'He was married,' she replied quietly.

'But how...? When...? I mean, when did you know?'

'Not until a few weeks ago. I had no idea before that.'

'Why, the absolute swine!'

Helen glanced at her father and could see the barely controlled fury in his blue eyes. 'It's all right, Dad, I'm over the worst now. It was a shock when I found out...' She bit her lip to try to stop it trembling.

Her father was silent for a moment as if battling with his own emotions, then he stretched out his hand across the table and covered hers. She found the pressure from his hand infinitely comforting and she gave a faint smile.

'I had no idea, you know, Dad—I really didn't. He'd seemed reluctant to discuss getting married or engaged, but I'd accepted that. I knew he was under constant pressure in his job and I didn't want to add to that...but I did believe that he loved me...' she swallowed and hesitated.

'You don't have to tell me now, Helen, if you'd rather not.' Her father's tone was gruff.

She shook her head. 'I might as well—you have to know some time. It's probably best to talk about it and get it over with.'

She paused reflectively, and when she continued, her voice was steadier. 'I went up to Manchester on a nursing course, but I returned unexpectedly, two days earlier than scheduled. I took a taxi from the station and went to Giles' flat. They...they were there together, he and this woman whom I'd never seen before. It was dreadful, Dad,' she said, staring at the tablecloth as she spoke. 'I've never been so embarrassed in all my life. I left immediately. Giles came to see me that evening, and it was then that he told me—the woman was his wife, Barbara. They've been married for five years.'

'Good God! Where had he kept her hidden?'

'Apparently they'd had some difficulties in their marriage and they'd been living apart, although they weren't legally separated. Giles told me that he'd become more involved with me than he'd intended. Anyway, I won't bore you with all the gory details, but the main point is that he's gone back to his wife.'

Oliver stared at her and seemed to be having some difficulty in finding something to say, then at last he squeezed her hand and muttered, 'I'm sorry, my dear, I'm sorry.' Then, more positively he added, 'Quite honestly, I'd say you were better off without him...believe me, if he were here I'd break his bloody neck!'

'Oh, Dad,' she smiled, 'it wasn't like that...it was just one of those things. I shall just have to get over it. Anyway, that's one of the reasons I came home, to lick my wounds—and to see you, of course. And from what I've heard since I've been here, it sounds as if I was meant to come home, even if it's only to help sort things out.'

Oliver looked up quickly. 'Does that mean you've decided to take the job?'

She sighed restlessly. 'I suppose I might as well, perhaps just for a month, even though your partner doesn't seem too keen on the idea. Still, as you were saying, it wouldn't do to let him have it all his own way, would it?' With that she yawned and stood up.

'You look tired,' remarked her father.

'I am, it's been a long day. I think I'll get an early night, Dad, if you don't mind.'

'Not at all,' he replied. 'You carry on, we can discuss the practice tomorrow.' He stood up and moving round the table dropped a kiss on her forehead.

For a moment Helen rested her head against his shoulder. It really was good to be home. She was glad now that she had come, even if things hadn't turned out quite as she had expected.

Later, alone in the guest bedroom, she undressed and at last gave free rein to the thoughts and feelings which she had kept tightly under control all day. Although she had told her father what had happened between herself and Giles, she had only given him the briefest outline. She had imparted very little of the shock and subsequent anguish she had endured when she'd found Giles and Barbara in bed together at his apartment. Taking the slides from her blonde hair, she sat in front of the mirror and picking up her hairbrush began to brush her hair with long strokes. Even now, more than a month later, as she recalled the scene, the sense of betrayal was as piercing as it had been then, and as the agony hit her afresh her grip on the hairbrush grew tighter, the strokes harder, so that when she finally stopped, her head was smarting and tingling from the onslaught.

When Giles had tried to explain to her that he and his wife had agreed to a trial separation and that he had become more involved with her, Helen, than he had intended, she had been consumed by anger, furious with him for having lied to her. Then, worst of all, with his decision to return to his wife and attempt a reconciliation had come the pain, almost physical in its intensity; it had left her drained of emotion and utterly exhausted.

Finally, when it had become apparent

that she was to be expected to go on working alongside Giles in a professional capacity, she had rebelled and handed in her notice. It had grieved her to do so, for she had loved her job at St Luke's, but she knew she couldn't go on being in such close proximity to Giles.

Helen had fallen in love with Giles Patterson from the very first moment she had seen him. He had strolled on to the ward at St Luke's late one afternoon, asked her if there was any tea on the go and casually announced that he was the new surgical registrar.

From the moment Helen's eyes had met his dark, smouldering stare her love for him had grown, but with such an intensity that at times it had frightened her. It had almost been an obsession, and she had never known love could be like that.

Slowly she slipped between the crisp sweetly scented sheets and in a rare moment of self-indulgence allowed the memories to flood back.

Giles had been a smooth, sophisticated lover. From the very beginning of their relationship he had wined and dined her in the best restaurants, taken her regularly to the theatre and the ballet and generally introduced her to a very different world from the one she was used to. He had come from a wealthy, privileged background and his current lifestyle depended more on a legacy from a maiden aunt than on his salary as a registrar. He had wooed Helen with such expertise and finesse that it had left her helpless with longing, completely under his spell.

Then in a single cruel moment her world had crashed around her, the magic evaporated and the dream was over. Helen knew all she could do now, however impossible it seemed, was to pick up the shattered pieces of her life and start again.

She knew she would have her father's love and support through this difficult time, but it had been a sudden impulse that had prompted her to take the job as practice nurse, and she was still uncertain whether she'd done the right thing. She flicked off the bedside light and tried to settle down, but sleep eluded her as her troubled thoughts still chased each other.

Helen knew she would miss St Luke's and all her friends. She had had a highly responsible job on the surgical unit and, as her father had reminded her, she would shortly have been up for regrading. Her friend Jill, another sister in whom she had confided, had thought she was mad, giving up everything just because of a man. Only a year earlier Helen would have agreed with her. Now, after meeting and loving Giles Patterson, nothing seemed the same.

Restlessly she tossed and turned, then as she plumped up her pillow in desperation, she heard the sound of a car, and as the beam from its headlights illuminated her room she realised it was in the drive. The tyres crunched on the loose gravel, then it stopped, the headlights dimmed and the engine died. A door closed quietly and Helen found herself waiting for the inevitable ring on the doorbell, believing it to be yet another patient in trouble. All remained quiet, however, then she heard the click of the front door followed moments later by the sound of footsteps on the stairs, and she realised it was Stephen Brett returning from the emergency call to the Attrill boy. Even now he was making his way upstairs—to her bedroom.

With a sound that could almost have been a sob, Helen turned her face to the wall, then as the tears finally overflowed and trickled down her cheeks she buried her face in the pillow.

Life appeared very different the following day when she awoke to a soft, mellow autumn morning, the smell of bacon cooking and outside, the sound of a chain-saw.

Flinging off her bedclothes, she jumped out of bed and padded across to the window. The guest-room was at the front of the house overlooking the drive and a corner of the orchard. The man using the chain-saw appeared to be roped to one of the large old pine trees fringing the front wall of the garden. It looked as if part of the tree had crashed down and the man was felling the rest of it. He was dressed in a brightly coloured checked shirt and denims while his eyes, below a shiny yellow helmet, were protected by a visor. A youth with spiky hair and a bored expression stood at the base of the tree watching the man. As if he sensed Helen standing at the window, he looked up.

She stepped quickly back into the room, aware that she was only wearing a flimsy nightie, and grabbing her towelling robe from the back of the door she stepped on to the landing and ran lightly along to the bathroom, struggling into her robe as she went.

As she reached the bathroom door it was suddenly wrenched open and she almost fell inside, colliding head-on with Stephen Brett who was coming out.

'Oh!' She gasped in horror as she realised he was clad only in a towel tied round his waist.

He seened equally taken aback to see her, and for a moment they simply stared at each other. Then as his gaze flickered downwards Helen became embarrassingly aware that her robe was open, revealing her pink transparent nightdress. Hurriedly she pulled the edges of the robe together and, fumbling in her haste, eventually managed to tie the belt around her waist.

It was Stephen who found his voice first. 'I'm sorry,' he muttered. 'I'd got used to having the bathroom to myself in the mornings. Your father gets up so early.'

'I'd forgotten you were here,' admitted Helen, trying without success to avert her eyes. He seemed to fill the entire doorway, and as she stepped backwards to allow him to pass she was conscious

74

of his muscular arms and his chest with its covering of golden hair. Giles's skin had been brown and very smooth, but there was something virile and very masculine about this stranger who had invaded her home. Feeling a flush rise to her cheeks, she dropped her gaze.

'We seem to be making a habit of this, don't we?' he said quietly.

Startled, she looked up and saw that there was a gleam of amusement in the hazel eyes while his hair, still wet from the shower, clung to his head in crisp, golden-tipped curls.

'Making a habit of what?'

'Getting stuck in doorways.' He suddenly grinned, and it transformed his face.

In spite of her embarrassment Helen found herself grinning back. The situation was rather ridiculous. 'We'll have to work out a rota for the bathroom,' she said, trying to keep her tone light.

'Either that or remember to dress properly.' He nodded, then, holding his towel tightly, he crossed the landing and disappeared into his room.

When Helen went downstairs she found her father and Stephen at breakfast. Carefully avoiding Stephen's eye, she helped herself to toast and coffee and asked her father to pass the marmalade.

'Is that all you're having?' Oliver frowned at Helen.

'It certainly is,' she said calmly as she took a sip of her coffee. 'And I'm surprised at you, still indulging in all that cholesterol,' she added with a disapproving glance at his cooked breakfast.

'I've made many concessions to keeping fit.' replied Oliver, 'but I'm damned if I'm going to give up my morning bacon. I can't imagine anything more ghastly than having to chomp my way through a bowl of chipped cardboard and sawdust like Stephen does every morning.'

They all laughed, and with a grimace Stephen set his spoon down into his muesli just as Mrs Parkes came into the dining-room with a fresh pot of coffee and more toast.

Her rosy face beamed as she looked at Helen. 'Good morning, love. Did you sleep well?'

Helen nodded, but before she had a chance to reply Mrs Parkes rattled on, 'It's so good to have her home again, isn't it, Dr Meredith? And to think she'll be working here as well—who would have thought it!' Shaking her head, she set down the coffee pot in the centre of the room and bustled back to the kitchen.

An awkward silence followed her departure and Helen glanced quickly from her father to Stephen. A frown had replaced the smile on the younger man's face and as he carefully set down his cup he said quietly, 'Has it been decided that Helen should work with us, then?'

'Well,' Oliver noisily cleared his throat, 'Helen did say, last night after you'd gone out, Stephen, that she thought she might as well give it a month's trial. You don't have any objection, do you?' When Stephen didn't immediately reply, he blustered slightly, 'After all, Helen is an excellent nurse...'

'That was never in dispute,' Stephen interrupted. 'I'm quite sure her qualifications are impressive, but, as I said last night, my objections would be on the grounds of two members of a family working together in the same practice.'

'But, my dear young fellow, it happens all the time.' Oliver was quite red in the face by this time and his eyes glinted beneath his bushy grey eyebrows. 'There are many family-run practices—why, I know of several husband and wife teams, and I myself worked alongside my own father for many years.'

'Amicably?' Stephen raised one eyebrow.

'What? What do you mean?'

'Did you and your father work amicably together?' asked Stephen patiently.

'Of course we did,' said Oliver, then, catching Helen's eye across the table, he said, 'Well, most of the time we did...I suppose we did have our differences, but let's face it, you get that in any practice whether the staff are related or not.'

'My point exactly,' Stephen replied. 'There are quite enough differences of opinion between any group of professional people working together on a daily basis without the added ones of domestic trivia. However, as it looks as if everything has been decided and, although it would have been nice to have been consulted further, I can see I have little alternative but to accept your decision, Oliver.'

'I say, old man, there's no need to take that attitude!' Oliver looked alarmed. 'I'm sure we can work out a system that's satisfactory to us all.'

Stephen stood up. 'I don't doubt it, Oliver. And while we're on the subject, may I suggest we have a meeting, the three of us, to work out the details? Would lunchtime be convenient to you both?' He looked at each of them in turn and irrelevantly Helen noticed that his hair was still damp in places, but where it had dried it had straightened. When they both nodded in agreement he turned on his heel and strode from the dining-room.

As the door closed behind him Oliver said, 'Well, I don't know what he's getting so upset about.'

Thoughtfully Helen looked up. 'He may have a point, Dad. Let's be honest—it doesn't always work out for family members to work together, does it?' Oliver merely shrugged in a non-committal fashion and Helen continued without pursuing the point further. She knew from stories her mother had related that all had not been sweetness and light in the Meredith camp when her grandfather had been in practice with her father. 'What I was really coming to,' she said quickly, 'is that you and Stephen are partners now and we really shouldn't have fixed up my employment with the practice without his approval. So if you think this is going to cause any trouble then I think it would be better if

I made other arrangements.'

'Nonsense!' Oliver stood up. 'Stephen is being ridiculous. Now tell me, did you have any plans for this morning?'

'Well, I...'

'Good—I have Mrs Jenkins coming in to have her leg ulcers dressed and a couple of ear syringings. You could do those for me if you like.'

'You mean me to start today?' Helen stared up at him in dismay. She had fully intended having a leisurely morning strolling to the village, renewing old acquaintances, then gossiping over morning coffee with Mrs Parkes.

'There's no time like the present,' Oliver replied on his way to the door. 'Besides, if you get started right away it won't give young Brett a chance to change his mind. Oh, there is just one thing, Helen,' he paused with one hand on the door handle. 'Do you have a uniform?'

'I think I have a couple of old ones somewhere. I've brought very little with me, though. Is it all right if I send for the rest of my things, Dad?'

'Of course it is.' His gaze softened. 'As I told you last night, this is your home—it's where you belong.'

After he had left the room Helen sat on at the table for some time reflecting on what had just happened. She had a feeling she was going to have trouble with Stephen Brett, for not only had they got off to a bad start, but he had made it quite plain that he didn't want her working for the practice. He seemed to regard her as some sort of potential trouble-maker, and Helen knew if she wasn't careful she could have a battle on her hands.

With her father, on the other hand, it had been as if the mere fact of her agreeing to work for them had lifted a burden from his shoulders. He had made it plain that he hadn't relished the idea of having to adapt to a strange practice nurse as well as a new partner. For his sake she knew she would have to try and make things work out.

Leaving the dining-room, she went through to the kitchen and asked Mrs Parkes about her old uniforms. After a certain amount of rummaging about they finally found them in the linen cupboard, and after Mrs Parkes insisted on ironing one for her Helen went upstairs to change.

By the time she returned downstairs in the crisp navy blue uniform and with her blonde hair neatly secured under a white cap she was in a slightly different frame of mind. Although this was far from the leisurely break she had had in mind when she had decided to come home, it would probably be good for her to throw herself into some work. If she had too much time on her hands she would only brood about what might have been.

CHAPTER FIVE

One or two patients had already arrived for morning surgery and were sitting in the waiting-room. They eyed Helen with interest and answered her greeting with obvious curiosity. There was no sign of her father or Stephen, then as she glanced out of the window she saw her father outside talking to the man with the chain-saw.

After only a moment's hesitation she walked briskly through the waiting-room past the row of patients, into an adjoining passage, then pushed open the door of what had once been the snug. The room, as she had anticipated, was almost beyond recognition.

Instead of chintz curtains, slatted blinds covered the windows and in place of the squashy sofa and armchairs a large desk and filing cabinets took up most of the floor space. She was interested to see, however, that the desk, instead of facing the door, was positioned to the right with both chairs on the same side so that doctor and patient sat informally together without the desk forming a barrier between them. The working surfaces were meticulously tidy, and Helen noticed that a far corner of the room had been partitioned off as an examination area.

There were no personal touches about the room that could give any clue to the personality of its occupant, and momentarily Helen found herself wondering about Stephen Brett. Apart from the fact that her father had said he was a bachelor, she realised she knew nothing else about him. Could he be the son of a friend or colleague of her father, or had he simply answered an advertisement placed by Oliver Meredith in a medical journal?

With a final rueful glance at the room

that had once been the snug, Helen thought that, whatever the circumstances for his being there, it seemed as if he was there to stay, so she would just have to get used to the idea.

As she walked back into the hall her father was coming through the front door assisting Mrs Jenkins, a patient who had just arrived in the Age Concern minibus. Both dogs were in the hall getting under everyone's feet, and as there seemed to be a decided possibility of them tripping Mrs Jenkins, Helen shooed them into the sitting-room and shut the door.

When she returned, her father's eyes lit up at the sight of her in her uniform. 'Ah, Helen, you remember Mrs Jenkins, don't you? I was just telling her about you joining us.'

'Of course I remember.' Helen smiled warmly. 'Hello, Mrs Jenkins.' She followed them into the surgery, where she helped Mrs Jenkins to remove her outdoor clothing, then assisted her on to the examination couch before removing the dressings from her leg ulcer so that Oliver could examine her. Afterwards he took the trouble to explain to Helen that he had been having problems with Mrs Jenkins as the ulcer was showing no signs of healing.

Helen carefully applied new dressings, chatting as she did so to Mrs Jenkins, who remembered her from when she was a child. After she had helped the old lady back into the waiting-room to rest until her transport arrived, she went back into the surgery and told her father about a new spray and impregnated dressing she had been using in the hospital.

'We were getting excellent results,' she added as he looked up from his desk with interest. 'Would you like me to order some, then we could try it the next time Mrs Jenkins comes in?'

'Of course, I'm willing to try anything that might help. Now, Helen, would you ask Mr Jolliffe to come in? He's for ear syringing. I gave him some eardrops in the week to loosen the wax, so there shouldn't be any problems.'

Helen was kept extremely busy for the next hour or so with ear syringing, a further dressing, then a routine injection for pernicious anaemia which she administered to the patient in the office while Oliver Meredith was examining another patient in his surgery. Finally she removed the sutures for a patient who had recently undergone an operation for varicose veins.

During this time Helen had seen nothing of Stephen, then almost at the end of surgery a medical representative from one of the drug companies arrived.

'I say,' he said, straightening his tie and eyeing her appreciatively, 'I haven't seen you here before.'

'That's probably because today is my first day,' Helen replied lightly. She was more than used to the wheedling charm of medical reps, having dealt with more than her fair share at the hospital.

'What are my chances of getting to see Dr Meredith today?' he asked hopefully.

'He has a patient with him at the moment, but when he's finished I'll ask him if he'll see you. I'm not sure about Dr Brett, though.' She glanced into the waiting-room and saw that it was empty.

'Dr Brett?' The rep looked up, interested. 'I didn't know there were two doctors here.'

'He hasn't been here very long.'

'Is he from the mainland?'

'I'm not really sure, but yes, I think he must be.'

The rep looked thoughtful, then he said,

'It wouldn't by any chance be Stephen Brett, would it? I heard he was coming down south.'

Helen looked surprised. 'As a matter of fact, yes, that is his name. Why? Do you know him?' Suddenly she was curious.

'I should say so! First-rate chap. I met him when he was a houseman, but I haven't seen him for a long time. I believe he spent some time in Africa and then went into practice in one of the big inner city areas—Glasgow, I think it was.'

'Well, you certainly know more about him than I do,' replied Helen, then as her father's last patient came out of the surgery she added, 'Are you promoting anything in particular?'

'Yes, we have a new product for cystic fibrosis—we hope it's a more palatable way of presenting enzymes. The trials so far have shown good results.'

'Well, take a seat for a moment,' said Helen, 'and I'll see what I can do.' She tapped on the surgery door and went in. Her father was writing up an entry in the patient's records, but he glanced up as she came in.

'Is that the last, Helen?' He looked at her over the top of his reading glasses.

'Yes, but there's a rep to see you.'

Oliver sighed. 'Do you know what he's promoting?'

'Something new for cystic fibrosis, he said.'

'Well, I'll see him as long as he keeps it brief.' He glanced at his watch. 'But it's Stephen he should be seeing really. He has a patient with cystic fibrosis.'

'He says he knows Stephen.' Helen hesitated, then added casually, 'Did you know him—before he came here, I mean?'

'Not directly, but he's the nephew of William Brett who I was at medical school with. It was a strange coincidence really, for when I was toying with the idea of taking a partner I had a call from William asking if I knew of a position on the Island as his nephew Stephen wanted to come here to live.'

'I see,' said Helen, thinking the situation was much as she had imagined it, but as she went out into the hall to tell the rep he could go into the surgery she found herself wondering just why Stephen Brett had chosen the Isle of Wight.

As Helen closed the door behind the rep Mrs Parkes put her head round the kitchen door. 'Are they ready for coffee yet, love?'

she asked anxiously.

'Almost, I should think, Parky, although I'm not too sure about Dr Brett. I'll just go and see if he's finished.'

Stephen was standing in the doorway of his surgery talking to his last patient, a teenage boy whom he was instructing in ways of controlling his acne. As Helen appeared he raised his eyebrows in surprise, then as the youth disappeared clutching his prescription he commented, 'I see you haven't wasted any time.' He glanced down at the navy blue uniform fastened at the waist with her sister's silver buckle.

Something about his tone of voice made the colour rise to Helen's cheeks. 'My father asked me to assist him,' she replied.

'Did he?'

She thought she detected a faint edge of sarcasm and added swiftly, 'I was perfectly willing to do the same for you.'

'I thought all that was to be decided at the meeting,' he said curtly. 'I suppose there still is to be a meeting?'

'Of course.' Helen bit her lip. Was she never to have a civil conversation with this man? Then, remembering why she had come to find him, she said, 'There's a rep here. He's with my father at the moment, but he's promoting a new product for cystic fibrosis—apparently there's been a good reaction to it.' As she spoke she saw the interest flicker in his hazel eyes. 'I believe you have a patient with cystic fibrosis?'

He nodded. 'Yes, she's the daughter of the local vicar.'

Helen frowned. 'Surely you don't mean Mr Marsdon?'

'No—John Foxe is the vicar here now. It's his little girl I'm talking about—poor little mite. I'd welcome anything to make life more tolerable for her.' His face softened and for the briefest of moments Helen caught a glimpse of a tender, compassionate side to his nature.

'I'll send the rep in to you,' she replied briskly, then as Mrs Parkes appeared with a tray of cups, she added, 'Ah, here comes your coffee.'

Later when the rep had gone and the two doctors had gone out on their rounds Helen decided to make a quick trip into the village to buy some stamps. She changed out of her uniform into a pair of beige slacks and a red shirt, then, pulling a chunky cream sweater over her head, she whistled for the two dogs and pulled open the front door.

It was a bright morning and the deep green of the pines merged with the golds, russet and browns of the other trees against the startling blue of the autumn sky. Helen paused on the step and sniffed appreciatively. Although they were several miles from the sea the heady salty tang was always in the air.

Mrs Parkes had just taken steaming mugs of coffee to the two men felling the old pine, and as Helen approached them the older man took off his helmet and carefully placing the huge chain-saw on the ground nodded a greeting to her. He had a florid complexion beneath a thatch of grey hair, but his eyes were a bright blue.

'Morning, miss,' he said, picking up his coffee and encircling the mug with gnarled grimy hands. 'Pretty day.'

'Good morning,' Helen smiled. 'Yes, it is lovely, isn't it?' She glanced towards the youth as she spoke, but only received a surly stare. 'What happened to the old pine?' She nodded towards the old tree which by now looked quite pitiful with half its trunk cut away.

'It were them gales we had last month,' the older man replied. 'They did a lot of damage round here, and that's a fact.'

'It seems such a shame,' remarked Helen. 'Those pines have been there for as long as I can remember.' With that she called to Plummer, who was rooting around in a pile of fallen leaves, then walked on down the drive, past a yellow van parked just inside the entrance, its blue lettering proclaiming to the world that the man with the chain-saw was Walt Foster from Chale.

Helen strolled down the main street as Dyer's Mead slumbered in the unexpected warmth of the November morning. A few shoppers plodded home from the corner shop next door to the pub, the Crown, and one or two, recognising Helen, called out or waved to her. Suddenly she felt pleased as a warm sense of belonging spread over her.

The Post Office was on the far side of the pub, and as Helen hitched the dogs' leads on to a hook on the wall she noticed an empty pushchair. Ordering Plummer and Jason to lie down, she pushed open the door and a bell clanged noisily above her head.

Mrs Prescott, a large lady with grey hair tied into an untidy bun, beamed at her from behind the grille. 'Hello, Helen. I heard you were home. How are you, love?'

'My word—' Helen smiled a greeting '—I'd forgotten how fast news travels around here! I only arrived last night.'

'Be staying long, will you?' Mrs Prescott asked as she tore off the strip of stamps that Helen asked for. 'Or is it just a little holiday? I know how hard you nurses work—earn every penny, you do.'

'I'm not really sure of my plans yet,' Helen replied vaguely. She knew from experience not to give too much information to Mrs Prescott, who thrived on village gossip. As she picked up her stamps a sudden movement caught her eye and, turning, she found a small girl beside her. The child, about three years old, was really quite beautiful, with large dark eyes and black curls. She was playing with a toy pony and lowered her gaze when Helen smiled at her.

'Katy, where are you? Come here!' A young woman suddenly appeared from behind a rack of greetings cards and held out her hand. She was tall, with the same black hair as the child, but hers was long, tumbling over her shoulders. She was dressed in denims, a sweater and a dark green body-warmer, and as her gaze met Helen's she paused, stared, then gave a little cry of pleasure. 'Helen! Why, Helen Meredith!'

Helen stared back, then her eyes widened in recognition. 'Amanda! How lovely to see you. Why, it's been absolutely ages!'

'Hasn't it just! But what are you doing here? I thought you worked in London.'

'That's right,' Helen replied carefully, only too aware of Mrs Prescott's interest in this unexpected reunion. 'But at the moment I'm staying with my father.'

'I see. If you've finished your shopping I'll walk up the road with you.'

The two girls left the shop and Amanda put Katy into her pushchair while Helen unhooked the dogs. The little girl squealed with delight as Plummer pushed his wet nose into her lap, then Amanda said, 'It really is great to see you again, Helen. Have you got time to come home with me and have a spot of lunch? We've an awful lot to catch up on.' Her dark eyes sparkled as she spoke, and for a moment Helen was transported back to their schooldays when they'd shared many escapades. Since leaving school the two girls had drifted apart, and Amanda was quite right, they certainly did have plenty to catch up on.

But Helen glanced at her watch as she remembered the practice meeting. 'I'm sorry, Amanda,' she said, 'but I have to get back to the surgery.' When the other girl looked surprised she added, 'I didn't want to say in front of Mrs Prescott, but I'm not just staying with my father, I'm working there as well.'

'Really?' Amanda looked interested, and as they fell into step, she remarked, 'That means you're working for Stephen as well?'

'Yes, in fact it was his idea to have a practice nurse.'

'But I understood you were working in a London hospital. That's a far cry from a rural practice, isn't it?

'Oh, I'm only here temporarily. I...I just needed some breathing space.' She looked down in sudden confusion.

'Man trouble?' Amanda sounded matter-of-fact, and Helen was forced to smile.

'You always could read me like a book, couldn't you?'

The other girl flashed her a wicked smile, the smile Helen remembered so well from the past when Amanda had been trying to wheedle her way out of trouble.

'I can see we really do have plenty to catch up on,' Amanda remarked drily as she manoeuvred the pushchair down the kerb and they crossed the road towards the church. 'So who is he, then?'

'Past tense, if you please. It's all over now, and he was a registrar at the hospital.' Helen's mouth tightened as she spoke and she was only too aware of Amanda's sharp glance. In an effort to divert the conversation she said, 'Anyway, you're a fine one to talk! It looks as if a few things have been happening in your life since I last saw you,' She nodded towards Katy, who was still enthralled with Plummer.

'Er—just a few.'

'So what happened to the film contract? The last I heard you were going to be the next Brooke Shields.'

'So I was.' Amanda pulled a face. 'But I've had to put that idea on ice for a while. Something more important came along, you see.'

'It had to be a man,' said Helen with a laugh. There was something infectious about Amanda's humour that had already lifted Helen's spirits, making her forget her own problems. By this time they had reached the lych-gate of the church, and Amanda stopped and reaching down into her bag which was hooked on the back of the pushchair she pulled out a poster. 'However did you guess? Yes, of course it was a man. A most wonderful man—but then Katy and I are prejudiced. I say, are you sure you won't have some lunch? I only have to put this poster up in the church porch and then we're going home.'

'I'd love to, Amanda, I really would, but I daren't miss this meeting. Stephen would think I'd done it on purpose, and I'm already in his bad books.'

Amanda looked at her in astonishment. 'Are we talking about the same person? I can't imagine Stephen having any bad books.'

'Well, I can assure you he hasn't been too happy with me since I arrived. Do you know him very well?' asked Helen, trying to sound casual but intrigued by Amanda's apparent familiarity with the new doctor.

'We're all registered with him, and he's been marvellous with Katy. He's very popular in the village.'

'Yes,' said Helen ruefully, 'I rather thought he would be. He's even Plummer's favourite person at the moment. Well,

Amanda, I really must go, but I'd love to come and see you some other time, then we can have a really good natter.'

'Right, Helen. Listen—we have to make an appointment with Stephen soon, so maybe we could arrange something then.' Amanda turned into the church path.

' 'Bye, Amanda.' Helen turned to go, then paused and called after the other girl, 'Oh, where are you living? Are you up on this new estate?'

Amanda stopped, then slowly turned. 'No, Helen—I'm sorry, I thought you realised. I live over there,' she pointed to a large grey house in the lane behind the church. 'My husband is John Foxe, the vicar.'

Helen stood and watched in amazement as Amanda disappeared beneath the lych-gate. If her friend had told her she had married Batman she couldn't have been more surprised. Then as she turned and made her way down the road to High Pines something clicked in her mind and she remembered that Stephen Barett had told her that it was the vicar's daughter who had cystic fibrosis.

At High Pines Helen found that a light lunch had been prepared and left in the dining-room, and as she took her seat both her father and Stephen arrived. They helped themselves to freshly baked crusty bread and wedges of Cheddar, then Stephen produced a rough outline he had prepared for the new administration of the surgery. It included an appointment system not only for himself and Oliver but for Helen as well.

'Oh, surely that isn't necessary?' Oliver interrupted. 'Why, this morning Helen assisted me as and when I needed help. Surely she can do the same for you?'

'I disagree,' said Stephen firmly. 'If we're to have a practice nurse then we must set up a system for her. What you're suggesting, Oliver, just wouldn't work. For example, if Helen is in your surgery working for you and I needed her to assist with one of my patients, then the next patient was yours and so on, the poor girl wouldn't know whether she was coming or going.' He turned to Helen, who had kept silent up until then. 'Where did you see the patients this morning?' he asked.

'Apart from an injection which I gave in the office I saw the rest in Dad's surgery.'

'That's what I thought. Now, as far as

I'm concerned that simply doesn't save any time at all. Just think, Oliver, if Helen could see patients in a separate room it would speed up our surgeries no end.'

'I agree,' Oliver helped himself to more cheese, 'but where do you propose she goes? We're pushed for space as it is.'

'I know that,' Stephen smiled, and once again Helen was struck by the way his smile lit up his face. 'And don't think I'm not grateful for the way you've converted your snug for my surgery, but one thing that did occur to me was that there's a lot of wasted space in the office.' As the others looked up with interest Stephen warmed to his theme and continued, 'Supposing we divided the office into two, the larger part could be a treatment-room for Helen and the smaller part could still serve as an office with a reception hatch made through to the waiting-room.'

'It would take some work to do all that,' grumbled Oliver, who hated change or disruption of any description.

'I know that, and I anticipated your reaction,' said Stephen smoothly, 'so I took the liberty just now of phoning Frank Jones, the builder in the village.'

'And what did he say?' Oliver glared at Stephen.

'That he could do the whole thing next weekend with the minimum of fuss.' Stephen turned suddenly to Helen. 'What do you think, Helen? You've been very quiet.'

Helen swallowed and glanced at her father, who was sitting stony-faced. She knew she had to be careful what she said, for, although she felt Stephen's ideas were good, she didn't want to appear to be siding with him against her father. In the end she said, 'I like the idea of the treatment-room, but if I'm to be working in there I won't be able to answer phone calls from patients wanting appointments.'

Oliver nodded smugly and looked at Stephen. 'Good point,' he said. 'Had you thought of that?'

'Of course,' Stephen replied, and the smile disappeared from Oliver's face. 'We'd already agreed that if we had a nurse she was to do some reception work, but obviously she can't do both together. So what I propose is that we have some cards printed informing our patients of our new plans, the clinics, etc., and also telling them at what times they can phone for appointments. In that way Helen can arrange her surgeries and the times she'll be working in the office to suit herself.

'Well, you seem to have thought of everything,' said Oliver.

'Just a moment,' Helen interruped. 'My typing's not up to much. Who does your referral letters these days?'

'Oh, don't worry about that,' Oliver replied. 'Jean Reynolds still comes in a couple of times a week. Mind you, she was talking about retiring recently.'

'Well, that won't be a problem when we get the computer,' remarked Stephen, 'not if we get one with a word processor, that is.'

'For God's sake, man!' Oliver stood up. 'Aren't you making enough changes without this wretched computer!' With that he stalked from the room.

In the silence that followed Helen stole a glance at Stephen. He looked up, caught her looking at him and gave a slight shrug.

'Doesn't he realise I'm trying to make life easier for him?' he said with a sigh.

'He hates change,' replied Helen simply.

'I can understand that, a lot of people of his age do, but I have my future to consider as well.'

'He only has another couple of years or so before he retires.' Helen was aware that her voice had taken on a pleading note. 'He really doesn't want so much hassle now, and when he goes you'll be able to run things as you want.'

'I know that, and I know it probably seems to you as if I'm just trying to be awkward, but that's not the case. The way I see things, there are radical changes coming in the Health Service, and when they come we must be equipped to deal with them.'

'I agree with you,' said Helen. 'Don't forget I've just come from a busy NHS hospital and I've seen what's happening, but all I'm asking is that you take things a bit more slowly where Dad's concerned. After all, you've not done too badly in the twenty-four hours that I've been here, have you?'

'What do you mean?' His cool hazel eyes with a hint of indignation in their depths met hers.

'Well, you've got your own way over getting a practice nurse, a mutual appointment system and the clinics you wanted. Surely you can ease up on the computer for a while?'

'Aren't you forgetting one thing?' His jaw had tightened, and Helen frowned. 'I didn't have my say over who we employed as our practice nurse.'

'And if you had, it wouldn't have been me. Is that what you're saying?'

By this time Stephen had stood up, and as he stared down at her his eyes narrowed. 'I think I've already made my views clear on that matter,' he replied, then he added, 'Now, if you'll excuse me, I have one more visit to make.'

After he had gone Helen sat on at the table, then as she heard his car draw away from outside the window she picked up the plan he had made for the surgery and screwing it up into a tight ball she hurled it into the waste paper bin.

CHAPTER SIX

The house was quiet when Helen finally left the dining-room, and on going to the kitchen she learnt from Mrs Parkes that her father had gone out with the dogs.

'How did it go?' Mrs Parkes jerked her

head in the direction of the dining-room, and Helen, knowing she referred to the meeting, pulled a face.

'I should imagine,' she said, 'much the same as any other meeting in any other practice.' She helped herself to an apple from the bowl on the kitchen windowsill.

'Well, Dr Meredith didn't sound too happy when he went out,' remarked Mrs Parkes.

'Don't worry, neither did Dr Brett,' Helen replied with a grin.

'Oh, I hope they're not going to fall out—I do so like Dr Brett. I've really got used to having him around.'

Helen sniffed. 'Well, I should say if he wants to stay he should take things a little more slowly. You know my father—he doesn't like to be rushed, and that's just what Stephen's doing—rushing him into making changes that he doesn't even want.' She bit fiercely into her apple.

Mrs Parkes looked up from the chops she was trimming for the evening meal. 'And what about you, love? This'll be a big change for you, working here, won't it, after what you've been used to?'

Helen sighed and eased herself up to sit on one of the worktops. 'I know, Parky, and I must confess I'm not entirely happy about it. For a start it'll take me time to adjust to the country way of life again. I'd become so used to the hustle and bustle of city life and the fast pace of work on a busy ward, I'm not sure I can adapt to the quiet here. After all, you must admit nothing much happens in Dyer's Mead. But that isn't the only reason I'm not happy.' She paused, taking another bite of her apple, and Mrs Parkes looked up enquiringly. 'I just don't think it's going to work out,' she stated flatly.

'Whatever do you mean?' Mrs Parkes sounded indignant. 'Why, your father is delighted you're here.'

'Oh, I know that, but Stephen Brett isn't exactly thrilled with the idea—he doesn't think members of the same family should work together. Let's face it, Parky, I shall be working for him as well, and I've got a feeling he's taken a dislike to me.'

'Surely not, love! You're imagining it. Why, he gets on with everyone. They all like him in the village.'

'So I believe,' said Helen drily. 'Everyone seems to regard him as some sort of god. I wish I could share their enthusiasm. By the way, Parky, I met Amanda Bridges in the village this morning. I haven't seen her for years. I had no idea she was married. I couldn't believe it when she told me who her husband was. I would never have put Amanda with a vicar in a million years—she was the wickedest one in our crowd!'

'Of course, you two were at school together—I'd quite forgotten.'

'It's funny how things turn out,' mused Helen. 'When we were younger I was the one who was going to marry and have children, while Amanda was to be the career girl...it just shows you never can tell.'

There was silence for a moment, then Mrs Parkes said quietly, 'I'm sorry about you and Mr Patterson, Helen. Your father told me this morning that your relationship was over.' When Helen looked up in surprise she added quickly, 'I think he was afraid I might put my foot in it and upset you.'

Helen shrugged. 'It's OK, Parky, I've just got to get over it.'

'You mustn't think it's the end of the world, dear. You're young and attractive, and before you know it there'll be someone else, just you see.'

'The way I feel at the moment,' Helen

replied with a grimace, 'I don't ever want any more to do with men!'

'Ah, you may feel that way now, but...' Mrs Parkes' words were cut short by the sound of running footsteps, followed by a pounding on the back door. 'Good lord, whatever's happening?' she cried as the door was flung back on its hinges and the youth with the spiky hair stood in the doorway, his face chalk-white.

'What's wrong?' Helen eased herself down from the worktop.

'It's Mr Foster!' The lad's breath was coming in gasps. 'Come quick!' His bored expression had gone now, replaced by one of sheer panic.

'Oh, my—it's that wretched chain-saw! I knew something would happen with that monster,' said Mrs Parkes as the colour drained from her face. In a moment of shock they listened, and there was indeed only silence from outside.

Helen glanced round the kitchen, then she grabbed two towels from a pile of clean laundry. If there had been an accident with the chain-saw there would be a great deal of blood. Swiftly she followed the youth out of the back door through the kitchen garden and round the side of the house.

As they crossed the lawn she could see the figure of Mr Foster slumped against the front wall beneath what was left of the old pine. The silent chain-saw was on the ground beside him.

'Did he fall out of the tree?' she rapped out as they sped across the grass.

'N—no,' stammered the youth. 'He was just going to climb the ladder when he said he had a pain—then he fell down.'

By this time they had reached the still figure, and Helen rapidly assessed the situation. There was no sign of any blood, but his face was putty-coloured and as she knelt down on the damp earth and lifted his wrist she could find no signs of a pulse, nor did he appear to be breathing. There was a bluish tinge around the man's lips, and immediately she knew she was dealing with a cardiac arrest and that she had to act swiftly.

Remembering that both doctors were out, she turned to Mrs Parkes, who had followed them, instructing her to call an ambulance. Mrs Parkes turned and hurried into the house without question; she was more than used to dealing with an emergency.

Helen meanwhile had engaged the help

of the frightened youth, and between them they pulled Mr Foster clear of the wall so that he was lying flat on his back. Helen then linked her hands together and with the heel of the lower hand found the point on the man's chest just below his sternum and began to administer cardiac massage in the form of hard rhythmic thumps. She kept this up for some moments, then glancing up at the youth she said, 'I want you to carry on doing this.'

'But...but I can't...' he stuttered.

'Of course you can,' snapped Helen. 'Just do exactly as I did.' As she spoke she grabbed the two towels and pushed them under the man's neck, so tilting his head backwards, then checking that his airway was clear she pinched his nostrils and covering his mouth with her own began to breathe into his lungs. Pausing between breaths, she noted that the youth was making a brave attempt at heart massage. For several agonising moments their efforts seemed to be in vain, then as Helen once again took over the heart massage and just as she was feeling her own strength beginning to fail, the man gave a choking gasp and his chest began to rise and fall.

Helen paused, and as her own breath came in short sharp gasps she felt herself being lifted from behind in a strong, firm grip.

'It's all right, Helen—you've done it. Let me get to him now.'

The voice was comfortingly familiar, and as she jerked her head she found it was Stephen Brett who had lifted her, and for a split second of exhaustion, in utter relief, she leaned against him.

Then gently he put her aside and crouched beside Mr Foster, who although he had come round was now groaning with pain. Swiftly Stephen moved him into the recovery position while indicating for Helen to open his case which he had set down on the grass. Just as he was giving the injection of morphine that Helen had drawn up for him the ambulance swung into the drive in a blare of klaxons.

While Mr Foster was being lifted on to a stretcher and transported into the ambulance Helen looked round for the youth who had helped her. He was sitting on the bank beside the drive with his head resting in his hands. There was something so dejected about him that it touched her, and she walked over to him and gently put her hand on his shoulder.

'Is he dead?' he mumbled without looking up.

'No, he's alive,' she replied firmly. When he still didn't look up, she added, 'You did very well, you know. In fact, you helped to save him.'

He lifted his head and looked at her, and she could see tear-stains on his cheeks, grimy where he had wiped them with his dirty hands. 'He'll be all right, then?' he asked, and Helen noticed that his hands were shaking.

'We hope so. They'll get him to the hospital, he'll be well looked after. By the way, what's your name?'

'Kevin—Kevin Foster.'

She stared at him. 'Is he your father?'

The youth shook his head. 'No, he's me uncle.'

'I see,' Helen turned and seeing Mrs Parkes hovering at the edge of the lawn, said, 'Parky, could you get some hot, sweet tea for Kevin here? He's had a bit of a shock.'

The youth stood up, but hesitated.

'Go on,' said Helen. 'Go with Mrs Parkes.'

'I was thinking about me auntie. Someone

should let her know.'

'I'll do that,' replied Mrs Parkes firmly. 'I know Lena Foster. I'll give her a ring, tell her what's happened, and she can get into the hospital to see Walt. Now you come on indoors with me, lad, and we'll see about that cup of tea.'

Helen watched the two of them walk across the lawn towards the house, then she turned as Stephen suddenly called to her from the back of the ambulance.

'Helen, would you travel with him? They do have a defibrillator on board, but I'd like to be on the safe side. I'd go myself, but I'm on call until Oliver gets back.'

'Of course,' Helen pushed back her hair, suddenly conscious of how she must look, then after only a second's hesitation she took Stephen's outstretched hand. His fingers closed around hers. They were cool and strong, just as somehow she had known they would be, and, as he helped her up into the ambulance, for a moment she found herself standing very close to him. Then he jumped down, the doors closed and she turned her attention once more to her patient.

The hospital was about six miles from

Dyer's Mead. The ambulance arrived without incident and Walt Foster was duly installed in the Coronary Care unit.

Helen stayed long enough to make sure he was comfortable and out of immediate danger, then, as she was about to leave the sister's office, Mrs Foster arrived. She was a small, thin, anxious woman who ignored Helen, directing all her questions to the sister. When the sister glanced at Helen and it became obvious that she was about to introduce her and possibly explain the part she had played in the afternoon's drama, Helen caught her eye and very slightly shook her head. Leaving a very worried Mrs Foster to follow the sister into Intensive Care, Helen quietly slipped out of the hospital.

It wasn't until she stepped outside into a freshening breeze that whipped tendrils of hair across her cheeks and caused her to shiver beneath her sweater that it suddenly hit her that she was virtually stranded. She paused on the hospital steps and looked around, then just as she was thinking that she would have to go back inside and ring for a cab she saw him.

He was leaning against his car, the dark green hatchback, and was wearing his waxed jacket over his sweater and cords. He was watching her, and when she hesitated he raised his hand.

She was surprised to see him, and slowly she walked down the steps and crossed the car park to join him.

'I thought you might be needing a lift,' he said lightly as he opened the passenger door for her.

'Aren't you supposed to be on call?' She ducked her head and slid into the seat.

'Oliver came in just after you'd left—I told him what had happened and that I intended to come and pick you up.'

Suddenly, for no apparent reason Helen felt ridiculously pleased that it had been his idea. For a moment she had quite thought her father had asked him to come.

'How is the patient?' he asked as he took his own seat beside her and fastened his seatbelt.

'He's comfortable. I think he'll be all right.'

'You did a first-rate job back there,' he commented as he started the engine.

'With the help of young Kevin,' she replied.

'The young lad?'

'Yes—apparently he's Walt Foster's

nephew. I thought he was a bit gormless at first until he started helping, then he really surprised me. He did exactly as I told him and he did it well. Not only that, he seemed really concerned about his uncle.'

'That may be so, but the credit still goes to you. You handled things very well.'

Helen flushed at his praise and trying to cover her embarrassment she shrugged and said casually, 'It's all in a day's work, and it certainly wasn't the first time I've had to do it.'

He threw her a brief glance. 'I wasn't suggesting it was, but I would imagine that on other occasions you've had a crash team on the way. What happened today is not the average sort of event one would expect in Dyer's Mead.'

Helen smiled. 'It's funny really, I'd only just said to Mrs Parkes that it would take me some time to adjust to the quiet of Dyer's Mead, where I thought nothing ever happened!' She glanced out of the window and saw that they had left the busy town behind and were heading into the countryside between fields neatly ploughed and sown with next year's crops. 'I expect you find life rather different here as well.' She turned and glanced at him, noting the straight nose and firm jawline and the unruly lock of hair over his eyebrow.

'Different from what?' Taking his eyes from the road, he threw her an enquiring glance.

'Africa? Glasgow?'

'My, you have been doing your home-work!'

She felt the colour flood her cheeks again and, not wanting him to think she had any special interest in him, she hastened to explain. 'The rep told me—he said he knew you when you were a houseman.'

'That's right, he did.' Stephen paused. 'What else did he tell you?'

'Nothing really. Only that you worked in Africa and then came back to this country and went into general practice in one of the big inner city areas—Glasgow, he thought. What did you do in Africa?'

'I spent two years in the Sudan with Voluntary Service Overseas. It was both harrowing and uplifting.'

'I can imagine,' replied Helen briefly, then fell silent as they crossed the top of the downs and began the descent into a valley fringed with tall conifers. As more and more aspects of this man's character were revealed to her she found she was becoming increasingly curious and felt she wanted to know more.

'Why the Isle of Wight?' she asked suddenly, breaking the silence.

'What do you mean?'

'Why did you choose to come here?'

'I was born here.'

She stared at him in surprise. 'You're an Islander?'

'There's no need to sound so amazed.' He smiled briefly. 'I lived in the Isle of Wight as a boy, then my parents moved to Kent, but my grandparents still lived at Freshwater and I chose to spend all my holidays here. I always promised myself I'd live here one day. Something to do with one's roots, I would imagine.' He glanced at her again. 'How about you?'

'Oh, I'm an Islander—I was born here and both my parents were, although my grandfather Meredith came here as a young man from his native Wales. I love the Island.'

'Yet you chose to leave and work in London. Why was that?'

Helen shrugged. 'I don't know—the need to spread my wings, perhaps.'

'But now you've returned?'

'For the time being, yes.' Her reply was

guarded. 'I really haven't decided on any long-term plans yet.'

He, however, seemed persistent and continued with his questions. 'I gather from your father that you were working at St Luke's?'

'Yes. I did my training there then my stint as a staff nurse and finally as a sister.'

'You enjoyed it?' The question was casual and Helen was caught off guard.

'Oh yes, I loved it.' The silence that followed her statement was suddenly charged with tension, and as she realised the corner he had manoeuvred her into she held her breath as she waited for the inevitable question.

It didn't come, however. Instead he pointed down into the valley at the autumn blaze of colours, the rich russet of the bracken, the copper of a cluster of beeches and the deep umber of the patchwork of ploughed fields. Then as she relaxed and he returned both hands to the steering wheel she found her gaze drawn again to the beautiful shape of his hands and felt a quiver deep inside as, quite against her will, she realised that once again she was comparing him with Giles.

It was as if the two men were at opposite ends of the spectrum, so different were they in every aspect—in looks, build and temperament. It seemed the only thing they had in common was their profession.

While she was still musing on the differences they reached Dyer's Mead, drove up the drive of High Pines, past Walt Foster's empty van, and came to a halt at the front entrance.

Stephen switched off the engine, but made no attempt to get out of the car. Helen unclipped her seatbelt and glanced at him.

'Thanks for coming to get me,' she said.

'That's OK. It was the least I could do,' he replied.

He still made no attempt to move, and she began to feel uncomfortable, for there was a speculative look in his eyes as he watched her. In the end she opened her door and made to get out.

Then he spoke. 'Forgive me for being naïve,' he said quietly, and she stiffened, 'but if you were so happy in your job at St Luke's, why have you come back here?'

So she hadn't got away with it after

all, she thought, and quite suddenly she knew she didn't want to tell him why she had left. She didn't want to explain about Giles—she didn't even want him to know she'd left for personal reasons, so her reply was quite flippant. 'Suppose I was to tell you that as I too am an Islander I had the urge to return where my roots are?'

He didn't answer, and at last she turned her head and looked him. There was a strange expression in his hazel eyes—an expression she was unable to read.

'You could certainly try and tell me that that was the reason,' he replied, then leaning towards her he unexpectedly reached out his hand and ran the back of his fingers down her cheek. 'But I wouldn't believe you.'

She stared helplessly at him, utterly at a loss for words, then he turned abruptly and got out of the car.

Helen followed more slowly, and when they got inside the house she went straight to her room. She had to change for evening surgery, but, more important than that, she needed some time alone—some time away from that cool hazel stare of Dr Stephen Brett.

CHAPTER SEVEN

During the next two weeks many changes took place at High Pines. True to his word, Frank Jones the builder completed the conversion of the office over the weekend, then during the following week Helen's treatment-room was furnished and equipped. The office section also received something of a face-lift, with two new carousel filing units, one for each of the doctors, so that all patients' records were in one area where Helen could have easy access.

After a series of further, sometimes heated practice meetings where details were thrashed out, patients received printed cards with full details of the new appointment system which would now operate for both doctors and the practice nurse. They were also informed of the new clinics which were to operate in the afternoons.

Some patients were suspicious of the new arrangements and said so, but on the whole the general feeling was such that the service to the public was greatly improved. Relationships within the practice, however, would still have to be worked at, and all three were aware of the inevitable friction.

Oliver remained tetchy and somewhat comtemptuous, although as the new scheme got under way and he realised that a good deal of work, both clerical and practical, had been taken from him he mellowed.

Stephen was optimistic in the face of opposition, for he was still convinced that all the changes could only be for the better. His only reservation seemed to be having Oliver's daughter working with them.

And Helen, to her surprise, found she was beginning to enjoy her work. It was very different from what she had been used to, and whereas at first she had been convinced it wouldn't suit her, as the days passed she found she was becoming absorbed. The patients were interesting, and their problems provided challenges very different from those she had encountered in hospital life.

As far as she was concerned during those early weeks the only disconcerting fact about life at High Pines came in the shape of Stephen Brett.

She found she was constantly aware of him, and she hated herself for it. In the very early days of their acquaintance she had been forced to face the fact that if it hadn't been for Giles and her broken relationship she could quite easily have found Stephen very attractive.

As it was, she wanted no involvement and was prepared to go to any lengths rather than let one start. On the other hand, she was uncertain as to Stephen's reaction to her. On the surface he seemed to resent her presence within the practice, but when they weren't working, such as the day he had brought her home from the hospital, he had appeared very different, and Helen knew she would have to be careful if she was not to give the impression that she was giving him any encouragement.

She hadn't seen Amanda Foxe again until the morning she brought Katy for her check-up.

After Stephen had finished examining the little girl Amanda took her back to the waiting-room to settle her in her pushchair. Helen was busy in the reception area sorting through some new registration cards, but she stopped when she saw Amanda and smiled down at Katy.

'How is she?' she asked.

'Stephen's very pleased with her. He's given me a new prescription to help with her food.'

'I heard there was something new,' said Helen. 'Let's hope it'll be more pleasant for her to take than what she was having before.'

'I hope so—Stephen said it should make a difference to mealtimes. He's so good with her, Helen.' Amanda glanced up and her face softened. 'I say, when are we going to get together? Are you still as busy here?'

Helen hesitated. 'Well things are still pretty hectic, but it's calmed down a bit now that we've worked out the new appointment system and rotas.'

'In that case why don't you come for dinner one night next week? John would love to meet you.' Amanda paused and glanced over her shoulder as the door opened behind her and Stephen appeared. 'Oh, Stephen, I was just inviting Helen to dinner—why don't you come as well? John wants to talk to you again about the village cricket team. I think he's frightened you might change your mind about joining.' She glanced from one to the other. 'How about next Friday evening?'

'Thank you,' replied Stephen immediately, 'I'd love to come.' He looked pointedly at Helen.

For a moment she was lost for words. This wasn't what she had in mind at all. She had been looking forward to a cosy chat with Amanda about old times. The conversation within a foursome would be very different. Then she realised that Amanda was waiting for her reply and Stephen was staring coolly at her.

'You will come, Helen?' Amanda sounded anxious.

'Yes...yes, of course. Thank you, Amanda. I'll look forward to it,' she replied.

As Amanda and Katy left the surgery and Helen turned to go back into the treatment-room she thought that just for a moment she caught the ghost of a smile flitting across Stephen's features. Then she had no further time to speculate what he might or might not be thinking, for Lily Prescott arrived for her blood-pressure check.

Mrs Prescott was full of her usual gossip, and this continued while Helen set up her sphygmomanometer, positioned the cuff on the patient's arm and adjusted

126

her stethoscope. The reading showed the pressure to be normal, so Helen wrote out a repeat prescription for Mrs Prescott's usual Atenolol tablets. She was just about to go through to her father's surgery to ask him to sign the prescription when as a matter of routine she glanced back at her patient and asked, 'Is everything else all right, Mrs Prescott? No worries about anything?'

The woman hesitated long enough to prompt her to repeat the question. Still she dithered, and this was so out of character that Helen came back into the room and shut the door.

'There is something bothering you, isn't there?' Helen said quietly. 'Would you like to tell me about it?'

'Well, I suppose I should tell someone, but I'm sure it will go away in time.'

'What will go away?'

'This lump.' The woman's eyes darted about and Helen could see the fear in them.

'What lump? Show me where it is,' she said, keeping her tone as matter-of-fact as she could.

'Here.' Mrs Prescott indicated her left breast.

'How long has it been there?'

She shrugged. 'I don't know exactly—a few months, I think.'

'You really should have let Dr Meredith see it before,' said Helen firmly.

'I know.' The woman looked uncomfortable. 'But I could never quite bring myself to say it to him—then when I knew you were working here, I thought to myself, on my next visit for my blood-pressure, I'll just mention it. You don't think it's anything serious, do you, Helen?'

'I really don't know, Mrs Prescott, but let me have a look. Of course Dr Meredith will want to see it as well.'

Mrs Prescott sighed. 'That was what I was trying to avoid. It all seems a lot of fuss about nothing.'

'Well, let's hope that's all it is. Now, if you'll just slip off your cardigan and unbutton your blouse.'

Mrs Prescott did as she was told, then as Helen examined her she watched her with anxious eyes. 'It's such a little lump, I'm sure it can't be harmful.'

By this time Helen had found the lump, just above the left nipple. It was indeed small and very hard, like a pea.

'Just wait a moment, Mrs Prescott, and I'll ask Dr Meredith to come and have a look at it,' she said as she left the treatment-room.

She had a quick word of explanation with her father, who gave a sigh of exasperation at his patient's reluctance to confide in him, then he strode into the treatment-room.

After examining Mrs Prescott's breasts thoroughly he attempted to reassure her by explaining that he hoped the lump was a simple cyst and that he would. attempt to aspirate it.

She stared at Helen in dismay. 'What does he mean?' she whispered as he crossed to the sink to wash his hands.

'He's going to see if he can draw off some fluid from the lump,' replied Helen gently. 'Don't worry, it won't be too bad, and I'll stay here with you.'

Dr Meredith's attempts to aspirate the lump were in vain, and as he motioned for Mrs Prescott to get dressed he told her that he would arrange an appointment for her in Outpatients to see a consultant.

By this time Mrs Prescott was understandably very frightened, and it took all Dr Meredith's and Helen's skill to reassure her. Helen saw her to the door. 'Now you'll get an appointment from the hospital within the next day or so,' she explained. 'Do you have anyone who'll go with you?'

'Yes, my sister will go, and my nephew will take us there in his taxi.'

'Oh, yes, of course,' replied Helen, remembering the driver who had brought her from the ferry. 'Well, you get yourself home now, make a nice cup of tea and try not to worry. In most cases these lumps prove to be nothing at all, but we do need to be on the safe side.'

When she returned to the surgery her father was writing in Mrs Prescott's notes. 'Will this be a referral letter for Jean to do?' asked Helen, then added, 'She's not in until tomorrow.'

Oliver looked up. 'No, we won't leave it that long. Perhaps you could ring Mr Blake's secretary at the hospital and ask for a priority appointment.'

'Of course,' Helen turned to go into the office, then paused as her father added,

'I do wish these ladies would tell me sooner when they find something like that. You'd think with the cover that the media give these days they'd be only too eager to get something sorted out.'

'I think it's mainly fear that prevents them, but also, especially with older patients, there's still a certain amount of embarrassment. Lily only just managed to tell me about it, let alone you.'

Shaking his head, Oliver returned to his notes and Helen went to ring the hospital.

On Sunday, after one of Mrs Parkes' excellent roast lunches, Oliver, who was on call, took himself off to his surgery to catch up on his correspondence and his medical journals, and Helen announced that she would take the dogs for a walk.

Stephen got up from the table and stretched. 'Could you use some company?' he asked, adding, 'I could certainly do with some exercise. I shall be putting on weight with all this delicious home cooking!'

Helen had planned a quiet walk alone across the top of the downs and into the beech woods. She enjoyed solitary walking and for a moment the prospect of company disappointed her, but as it would appear churlish to refuse and as Plummer, who had heard the word 'walk', was jumping excitedly around Stephen, she merely smiled and nodded. 'Just give me a moment and I'll fetch an anorak,' she said, and slipped out of the room.

As she hurried upstairs she had to admit that she and Stephen did seem to be getting on a bit better, although he still seemed to have his original reservation about her working for the practice. He had, however, seemed quite satisfied with her methods of working and she had found his ways, although quite different from her father's, equally admirable. Where Oliver Meredith adopted the policy of remaining slightly aloof from the patients in his professional capacity, Stephen seemed to positively encourage social contact, the use of Christian names and the consequent building of an easy rapport between doctor and patient.

He was waiting for her in the hall and as she came down the stairs he glanced up. Their eyes met and she detected a spark of admiration in his. She was wearing cream cords which she had tucked into her boots, a thick patterned sweater and her anorak. Her blonde hair she had caught up on either side of her head with two Japanese combs.

'Ready?' He smiled and whistling for the dogs opened the front door.

As they tramped through the furrows of fallen leaves on the path to the downs

Helen remarked that the first chill of winter seemed to be in the air.

Stephen nodded. 'I always think,' he said, 'that there's something a little sad about the passing of autumn, but then when winter arrives I usually enjoy it. There's something to be said for log fires, roasting chestnuts and Christmas.'

As they climbed the steep chalk pathway the scent of woodsmoke rose from the valley below, but when they reached the crest of the downs the air became clear and sharp and they quickened their pace across the short springy turf to keep up with the dogs, who, with their noses to the ground, forged ahead.

The path dropped sharply and almost disappeared into a sea of dead bracken, crisp and curled like bacon rind, and they were forced to walk in single file until they entered the stillness of the beech wood. Their feet rustled and stirred the copper carpet, while the smooth grey trunks rose majestically above like the pillars of some great cathedral.

Plummer flung himself into a bank of dead leaves in an ecstasy of delight, while Jason, more dignified, nuzzled the roots of one of the giant trees. Helen and Stephen paused to watch, amused by the antics of the two dogs.

'How quiet it is here,' said Stephen as he gazed up through the sparsely clad branches of the beeches.

'This has always been one of my favourite places,' replied Helen.

'Because of the peace?'

'I'm not sure.' She hesitated and reflected, then realised that yes, she did feel a true sense of peace—the first she had really known since Giles had left. She glanced at Stephen and saw that he was looking down at her enquiringly, almost as if he expected her to enlarge on her reply. 'I suppose it's just always been a special place,' she added.

'Special memories?'

'Yes, childhood memories, that sort of thing.'

They walked on in companionable silence, and she was suddenly struck by how easy it was to be with Stephen, especially when they were away from work. It hadn't been like that with Giles. He had always been so full of enthusiasm, demanding that they do somewhere different, try something exciting or find a new experience. Stephen seemed content simply to walk in silence by her side.

She threw him a glance from under her lashes. The chill had brought a healthy glow to his cheeks while the last of the afternoon sun, which filtered through the branches of the trees, picked out the glints of gold in his hair.

'Did you play in these woods as a child?' he asked suddenly.

'Sometimes, but mostly I came here with my mother.'

'Ah, yes, your mother. You must miss her a lot. How old were you when she died?'

'Fifteen,' Helen replied, thinking how easy it was to talk about it to him. Most people evaded ever asking about her mother, and consequently, over the years, Helen had kept her thoughts to herself, locking them away with her memories.

'Hm, a pretty vulnerable age, I would imagine, for a girl to lose her mother.'

'It was,' Helen replied briefly, at the same time reflecting that Giles had not once asked about her mother. She glanced at Stephen. 'What about your parents? You said they moved to Kent when you were a boy—do they still live there?'

'My mother does.'

'Isn't your father alive?'

'Oh yes, alive and well and living in Buckinghamshire.'

'Are they div...'

'Divorced? Yes, and they've both re-married.'

A strange, almost shuttered look had come over his face, and Helen hesitated before asking, 'Is your father a doctor?'

'He is.'

'I thought he might be. I knew your uncle was, he was at medical school with my father.'

'My mother's a GP as well.' Again the shuttered look spread over his face.

'Really?' Helen paused. For some reason it surprised her that his mother was also a doctor. 'Were they in practice together before they divorced?'

'They were.' His reply was terse, and she threw him a sharp glance.

'Would that by any chance have anything to do with your aversion to members of the same family practising together?'

'It has everything to do with it.' Stephen took a deep breath. 'It was a disaster, and I'm sure it was what led to the final break-up.'

136

'How old were you when they parted?'

'Seventeen.'

'Did it affect you very much?'

When he didn't answer immediately Helen wondered for a moment if she'd gone too far with her questions. She wasn't usually a nosey person, but suddenly she'd wanted to know about him; it had become important to learn about his background and his life before he'd returned to the island he loved so much.

He sighed. 'If I'm honest,' he said slowly, 'yes, it did affect me.'

'But surely you still see them both?'

'Yes, sometimes. But it's never been the same. I'd always considered myself to be close to both my parents in spite of all the arguments at home, but since they've parted, and especially since they've remarried, I don't feel that I belong with either family. Both my step-parents had other children younger than me and I didn't seem to fit in.'

They walked on in silence, then Helen said, 'I can understand how you feel, but I don't believe that you can base your prejudice on that one incident. Just because your parents couldn't work together it doesn't follow that that would happen in every working relationship. I've always got on well with my father.'

'But you give in to him regularly,' said Stephen mildly.

'I do not!' Helen's reply was indignant.

'But you don't like to upset him, do you?'

'Well, no, I suppose I don't, but I happen to be very fond of him.'

'Exactly...because he's your father. If he weren't I've a feeling you'd be far more outspoken over practice matters.' He stopped and with his hands on his hips he stood in the middle of the path and surveyed her, a half smile on his lips. 'Come on, admit it. I'm right, aren't I?'

'Well, I...' Helen looked away, embarrassed.

'I'll bet you were far more strict on the wards, weren't you, Sister Meredith?'

Finally she was forced to laugh. 'Yes, I suppose I was,' she admitted ruefully.

They walked on and Stephen threw a stick for Plummer, who dashed off, ears flying, to retrieve it.

'I wonder why it is,' he said thoughtfully, 'that people always seem to be inhibited by their parents. It's something that fascinates me. I fancy the majority of people behave in a vastly different way when in the company of their parents than they would normally.'

They paused as Plummer came crashing back and, dropping the stick at Stephen's feet, sat gazing up in adoration waiting for him to throw it again.

'What ward were you on at St Luke's?' he asked, changing the subject after he'd hurled the stick once again.

'I was on the surgical unit, it was a very busy ward,' Helen replied guardedly, wondering just where this conversation would lead.

'And how are you finding that general practice compares with it now that you've had a couple of weeks to settle down?'

'Well, it's very different, of course, but I can't say I'm not enjoying it.'

'Do you think you'll stay?' He asked the question casually and she threw him a sharp glance. His expression, however, gave away nothing.

'Surely that partly depends upon you?' She hesitated. 'You may not find my work satisfactory.'

'I shouldn't think that's very likely—from what I've seen you're very efficient.'

She felt a sudden glow touch her cheeks,

and it had nothing to do with the chill of the late autumn afternoon.

The path at that point in the woods suddenly rose sharply and tramping through great troughs of leaves they climbed to the top of the incline, and as the trees thinned out they stood for a moment looking down at the fields below and the bridle path that skirted the copse and which would eventually take them back to the village.

It was as they began to descend the bank that a sudden gunshot sounded in the distance and Plummer surged forward, barking madly. He careered in front of Helen, who missed her footing and stumbled, flinging out her arms to save herself.

Stephen, who was slightly ahead at the foot of the bank, heard her sharp cry and turned just in time to catch her and prevent her falling headlong.

Gasping for breath, Helen leaned against him. After a few moments she lifted her head, but he didn't release her. Instead his arms seemed to tighten around her, drawing her even closer. She could hear the steady beating of his heart beneath his sweater and for a moment she felt comfortable and safe within the shelter of his arms and had no immediate desire to move. When she eventually lifted her head again she found herself staring up into that cool hazel stare, then as her gaze flickered over his face, coming to rest on his full, firm lips, he lowered his head and before she had the chance to protest his mouth covered hers.

It started as a cool, light, almost leisurely kiss, then as his arms tightened yet again, Helen found herself responding, her lips opening beneath his as a sudden surge of desire swept through her, striking a chord deep inside and reawakening a passion she had thought had died forever.

When at last they finally drew apart it was difficult to tell who was the more surprised. For a moment Stephen looked embarrassed, and to cover it he made a show of whistling for Plummer, who seemed to have disappeared, quite unaware of the havoc he'd caused. Jason, however, was sitting watching them with obvious interest, his head on one side, his tail thumping the ground.

In silence they took the bridle path, and it was not until they were almost halfway back to the village that Stephen spoke. Clearing his throat, he said, 'I owe you an apology—I'm sorry, that shouldn't have happened.'

Helen was about to tell him not to worry about it when he continued speaking, not giving her a chance to interrupt.

'Your father told me that you're practically engaged—I shouldn't have taken advantage.'

She stiffened and threw him a glance. 'When did he tell you that?' she asked, trying to sound casual.

He shrugged. 'I'm not sure. Soon after we went into partnership, I think.'

Helen took a deep breath. So Stephen didn't know about her break-up with Giles. She opened her mouth to explain, then shut it again as he said, 'He's a surgical registrar, isn't he?'

She nodded. 'Yes, at St Luke's.'

They walked on in silence, and somehow the moment was lost and Helen found that she couldn't bring herself to tell him.

Then, as the village came into sight below them with the smoke from cottage chimneys rising straight up into the already darkening sky, she suddenly decided that it might be as well if Stephen were to believe that she was still involved with Giles.

She had a strong suspicion that if he knew otherwise he might try to start a relationship with her, and she didn't feel she was ready for that. There, had, however, been something intriguing, exciting, about his kiss, and she knew that she could find him very attractive if the circumstances had been different. As it was, she had been so badly hurt by Giles that she felt her emotional judgement might be impaired, and any relationship started now could surely only be on the rebound.

CHAPTER EIGHT

The following week proved for Helen to be just as busy, with yet another new clinic being set up on the Wednesday afternoon. This was an ante-natal clinic and was run in co-operation with the community midwife. In the past, ante-natal appointments had been arranged during surgery times and it hadn't always been possible for the midwife to attend. The new system promised to be easier for all concerned: doctors, midwife and the mums-to-be.

It was Helen's responsibility to deal

with the patients' records, to talk to them about any worries they might be having, whether medical or social, to check their weight, take their blood-pressure and check their urine for any traces of sugar or albumen. She had also, together with the midwife and area health visitor, arranged for relaxation and parentcraft classes to follow the ante-natal clinics.

As the last of the expectant mums were chatting together over a cup of tea in the waiting-room and Helen had just said goodbye to Susan Jefferies, the midwife, she noticed a small, thin-faced woman sitting in the corner of the waiting-room. She was clutching a large pot of yellow chrysanthemums and quite obviously, by her age, wasn't an ante-natal patient. There was, however, something familiar about her, although for a moment Helen couldn't remember where she had seen her.

'Can I help you?' asked Helen as the woman stood up.

'Are you Sister Meredith?' The woman sounded anxious.

'Yes,' Helen smiled. 'I'm sorry, have we met?'

The woman shook her head. 'I'm Lena Foster—you helped my husband when he was taken ill. I...we...wanted to say thank you.'

'Why, Mrs Foster, how kind!' said Helen as the woman, clearly overcome, thrust the plant into her hands. 'How is your husband?'

'Well, he's still in the hospital, but they say he's going along nicely...but if it hadn't been for you...well, I dread to think what might have happened. Our Kevin told me what you did, and I wanted you to know how grateful I am.' She glanced down at the plant. 'I know it doesn't seem much, but I didn't know what else to do...'

'You didn't need to do anything,' replied Helen quietly. 'I'm just pleased your husband is recovering. Give him my kind regards, and thank you for your kindness.'

Mrs Foster nodded and turned sharply, almost colliding with Stephen, who watched her walk hurriedly away.

'Who was that?' He glanced at Helen.

'Mrs Foster,' she replied, 'Walt Foster's wife. You remember, the cardiac man.'

'Ah, yes. How is he?'

'Still in hospital, but improving, apparently.'

'Good.' He glanced at the plant in her

arms. 'It looks as if you're the flavour of the month around here at the moment!' He grinned. 'All the mums have been singing your praises this afternoon.'

As his amused gaze met hers Helen felt the colour stain her cheeks—she still found it difficult to accept praise from Stephen.

Two days later Helen had to take some specimens to the pathology lab at the hospital and pick up some shopping in town. Stephen, who had a patient in the gynae ward, offered to drive her to the hospital.

It was a grey, overcast morning when they set out soon after morning surgery. A cold wind whipped up the dead leaves on the drive, tossing them into the air in miniature whirlwinds, and Helen shivered and turned up the collar of her raincoat as she took her seat beside Stephen.

He had seemed rather distant towards her since the incident on their walk, and while on the one hand she was relieved, on the other she was anxious that the friendly relationship that appeared to have been developing between them might have been jeopardised.

At the hospital she arranged to meet Stephen in the coffee shop in the foyer in half an hour's time. She watched him stride off down a corridor towards the gynae wing and two nurses, who passed him, nudged each other and turned to stare after him. It struck her more forcibly than ever just how attractive he was, then with a little shrug she turned towards the path lab.

She had delivered her specimens in a matter of minutes and, realising she had at least twenty-five minutes to wait for Stephen, on a sudden impulse she made her way towards the Coronary Care Unit. After a brief word with the sister in charge, who fortunately recognised her, she was shown into the ward to see Walt Foster.

He was sitting in an upright chair beside his bed, and his pleasure at seeing Helen was more than obvious. He looked comparatively well, and he gripped her hand tightly as his ruddy, weather-beaten face broke into a smile.

'It does me good to see you,' he said. 'Me and my missus were only sayin' we didn't know how we could thank you for what you did.'

'I was glad to be there at the right moment,' said Helen, and added, 'Your wife came to see me and brought me a beautiful chrysanthemum.'

'Aye, that were one of mine—I grow them for a hobby,' he said proudly.

'Well, it was very kind of you both, and I shall look after it carefully,' Helen smiled, touched by the man's honest gratitude.

'Will you be staying, Sister?'

'Staying?' Helen looked puzzled, thinking he meant on the ward.

'In Dyer's Mead?' He leaned forward, a look of interest on his features as he waited for her reply.

'I'm not sure yet.' She hesitated. 'I haven't quite decided on my future plans.'

'Well, I think the surgery's a better place for you being there, and that's a fact, and it ain't only me who says so—there've been several in from the village to see me and they all agrees with me.' Walt leaned back, tired but satisfied with his pronouncement, while Helen left the ward with warm glow inside her and Walt's words ringing in her ears.

Stephen was already in the coffee shop and had ordered for them both. He stood up as she approached the table and almost as soon as she sat down a waitress brought their coffee.

'Sorry if I've kept you waiting,' she

said breathlessly, 'but I went to see Walt Foster.'

'How is he?'

'He's looking very well. I would say he's on the mend. Have you seen your patient?'

He nodded, thoughtfully stirring his coffee.

'Do you often visit your patients in hospital?' asked Helen curiously.

'Not usually, but this was an exceptional case. The patient had been admitted for a cone biopsy of the cervix following a positive smear test. It proved to be malignant and Mr Mahmoud has performed a total hysterectomy. Unfortunately it was too late, it had spread well into her pelvis.' He stared into his cup. 'It's very sad, she's only in her thirties and has three children. The prognosis is not good.'

'How long?' Helen enquiried quietly.

'Two years at the very most.'

'Does she know?'

He looked up, and as her eyes met his she glimpsed the tension and concern there. 'That's what I came in for to today—to tell her and her husband. The registrar felt it would be easier coming from me.'

'I'm sorry, Stephen. How did they take it?'

He shrugged lightly and looked away. 'Who knows? How does anyone cope with that sort of thing?' He gave a deep sight. 'I always feel inadequate afterwards, wondering if I could have handled it differently—softened the blow in some way.'

'I'm sure you did all you could,' said Helen, suddenly filled with a surge of admiration for the compassion in Stephen. She'd seen enough of the medical profession to know that compassion wasn't necessarily a built-in characteristic.

He remained silent for some moments, and it was Helen who finally broke the silence when she said, 'What you've just told me endorses our feelings about holding more cytology clinics, doesn't it?'

He nodded, and as he stood up, he said, 'Talking of that, did Maureen Arnold make her appointment?'

Helen smiled. 'Yes, she's coming to one of my clinics.'

'Good.' He glanced at his watch. 'Now, we'd better get into town, and while you do your shopping, I'll get a bottle of wine to take to the Vicarage tonight.'

'Good idea,' Helen replied as she followed him from the hospital, but as she thought of the dinner party that evening a twinge of apprehension shot through her. She knew Amanda of old and she had a feeling her friend was up to something.

When they left High Pines that evening to walk the short distance to the Vicarage the wind had dropped and it was a calm, still night. Mrs Parkes had seen them off with a smile and a wave and Oliver had called out from the drawing-room as they passed, telling them to enjoy themselves, for all the world as if they were embarking on a date together.

Amanda had stipulated casual dress, but Helen had found herself taking extra care over her appearance. She had tried several outfits, but nothing had seemed quite right, then finally she'd settled for a full black shirt in a soft material that accentuated her slim waist and teamed it with an emerald-green blouse. Her hair she left loose, and after she had added a pair of jet earrings and matching beads she felt satisfied.

She wasn't sure why she had gone to so much trouble. It couldn't be for Stephen's benefit, she told herself firmly, for hadn't she already convinced herself that she didn't want a relationship with him—or with any man, for that matter? She still felt too bruised and raw after Giles to trust anyone else—but as she glanced in her mirror for a final check she noticed that her eyes were sparkling in a way they hadn't done for some weeks.

And in spite of all her good intentions the memory of Stephen's kiss had stayed with her, haunting her dreams and intruding into her everyday thoughts at the most unlikely moments. There had been something deeply satisfying about the kiss, but at the same time it had held a promise of something more, some latent sensuality that Stephen Brett kept well hidden in his cool, day-to-day approach.

He'd been waiting for her in the hall, casually dressed in rich brown cords, a cream shirt and a tan-coloured leather jacket. He had obviously tried to tame his hair, but still it waved, the one unruly lock falling forward. His eyes had lit up with admiration as he had taken in her own appearance.

They were mostly silent on the walk through the village, then as they turned in to the lane alongside the church, thick yew trees on one side and the dark outlines of ancient tombstones on the other, Stephen asked, 'How well do you know Amanda?'

'We were at school together. In fact, we used to be great friends, but we'd lost touch recently.'

'Were you at school here on the Island?'

'Yes, it was a private girls' school, but we were day girls.' Helen glanced at his profile illuminated by the lamp on the edge of the church. 'How well do you know them?'

'Only really since I've been here and they registered with me, although I had met John Foxe before; he'd been involved in some missionary work when I was with VSO and we were introduced just before I went to Africa. You'll like him, he's a great character.'

'I must admit I'm curious,' said Helen as they reached the Vicarage, a large grey stone Victorian house. 'I still find it hard to imagine Amanda married to a vicar.'

'Ah, but John Foxe is no ordinary vicar,' replied Stephen as he pulled the brass bell chain.

His words proved to be right, and from the moment John Foxe opened the door to them Helen took an instant liking to him. Dark-haired and bearded, he towered above her, while his warm brown eyes behind heavy horn-rimmed spectacles seemed to be smiling even when his mouth was not. Dressed in a polo-necked sweater and Levis, he hardly looked like a man of the cloth, but it became obvious to Helen in a matter of minutes why Amanda had fallen for him. His enthusiasm and charm made them feel instantly welcome, and as he led them into the comfortable book-lined sitting-room and poured drinks for them, explaining that Amanda was putting Katy to bed, Helen felt as if she had known him for years.

Amanda appeared as they were sipping their drinks, looking vibrant and slightly exotic in a scarlet gypsy-style skirt, white blouse and with her thick black hair caught up high on her head so that the mass of it tumbled about her shoulders. Stephen stood up and she touched his hand in greeting, then, including Helen, she said, 'Lovely to see you both. I'm so pleased you could come.'

'May I get you a drink, darling?' Her husband turned from the sideboard and gave her a look of such love that Helen felt a pang of envy.

154

'Please.' Amanda returned the look, then turning to Stephen, she said, 'I'm sorry, Stephen, but Katy's had rather a bad day, she knows you're here and she's saying she won't go to sleep until she's seen you.'

Stephen smiled and set down his glass. 'In that case, I'd better go—mustn't keep a lady waiting!'

He walked towards the door, but paused as Amanda said, 'Oh, Helen, could you go up as well? She wants to ask you about Plummer.'

Helen followed Stephen upstairs and into Katy's nursery. The little girl was in bed, but her large dark eyes were turned expectantly towards the door. To Helen's surprise she lifted her arms to Stephen, who immediately crouched down alongside the bed and gave her a hug, dropping a kiss on to the shiny black curls.

'Hello poppet,' he said softly. 'How have you been today?'

'I coughed and I was sick,' she replied solemnly.

'But are you better now?' he persisted gently.

She nodded, then looked over his shoulder to where Helen hovered near the door.

Stephen straightened up and turned to Helen. 'Look, Katy, I've brought Helen, Plummer's mistress, to see you.'

'Is Plummer with you?' The dark eyes widened and tried to see beyond Helen on to the landing.

'No, he's at home in bed,' Helen explained.

'Oh!' The child's face dropped in disappointment.

'He was very tired, he'd been rushing around all day,' Helen said hastily, then added, 'But I tell you what, if you're still poorly tomorrow, I'll pop in to see you with Plummer when he goes for his walk.'

'What about if I'm better?' demanded Katy, and Helen glanced at Stephen as a grin crossed his features.

'Then you can come and see Plummer when you go shopping with Mummy,' she replied quickly.

The child seemed to accept these arrangements and snuggled down under her Peter Rabbit duvet. They stayed for a few more minutes talking to her about her pictures and toys, then her eyelids grew heavy and they crept from the room and joined her parents downstairs.

They ate dinner around the pine table in the vast flagstoned kitchen. The room, quite obviously the hub of the household, was cosy and warm with two rocking chairs in front of the Aga. Bunches of dried flowers and herbs hung from the ceiling and filled copper and earthenware jugs that stood on the windowsills and around the hearth, while Katy's paintings adorned the walls.

Amanda had prepared a smoked mackerel starter followed by a delicious vegetable lasagne and a salad. If Helen had had any doubts over the nature of the conversation they were quickly dispelled as John seemed to guide them from one topic to another and they ended up discussing everything from bee-keeping to sailing at Cowes.

'Are you going to buy a boat before the season, Stephen?' he asked as he leaned forward to refill their glasses with his excellent home-made barley wine.

'I'd certainly like to,' Stephen replied, glancing at Helen as she looked up in surprise.

'I didn't know you were into sailing,' she commented.

'Oh, yes,' he replied. 'I've enjoyed it since I was a boy—my parents kept a thirty-footer down at Burnham.'

'You sail, don't you, Helen?' asked Amanda, looking from one to the other with sudden interest. 'I remember joining you and your father in the old days for the odd trip round the Island.'

'Yes,' Helen smiled. 'You were always sick. I spent most of the time holding a bucket for you!'

Amanda pulled a face and the men laughed. 'Do you still sail?' asked John.

'I haven't sailed for a long time, but Dad still keeps a boat at Bembridge.'

'Well, if Stephen buys a boat you'll be able to crew for him,' said Amanda innocently, but there was a wicked gleam in her eyes that confirmed Helen's earlier fear that she was up to something. Slightly embarrassed, Helen lowered her gaze, but not before she'd noticed Stephen's amused look.

'I think,' he said, 'I'd better concentrate on finding somewhere to live before I worry about buying a boat—I can hardly go on sleeping in Helen's bedroom forever.'

A stunned silence followed his words, then as Helen felt a telltale flush touch her cheeks, Amanda raised her eyebrows and John threw back his head and roared with laughter.

'I won't ask you to explain yourself further, Stephen,' he said at last. 'But, talking of looking for somewhere to live, have you heard that Heron Cottage is about to come on the market?'

Stephen narrowed his eyes. 'Heron Cottage? Isn't that old Sam Bartholomew's place down by the creek?'

'That's right,' John replied. 'Poor old Sam's been in hospital for several months now and won't be able to look after himself when he comes out. I've persuaded him to go into a residential home where he'll be properly cared for. He wasn't too keen at first, then he saw the sense of it and agreed to sell his cottage. It's in the local agent's hands—why don't you go and have a look at it? You must know the place, Helen?'

'Oh yes, I know it well,' she replied. 'My mother used to visit Mrs Bartholomew when she was ill and I used to go with her. It's a wonderful place, full of nooks and crannies, and of course the position is marvellous down there overlooking the marshes.'

'It sounds just what I'm looking for,' mused Stephen, carefully paring an apple

159

as he spoke, and once again Helen found her gaze drawn to his hands, watching the deft movements of his strong fingers. 'It sounds quiet, but at the same time it's not too far away from the surgery.'

'And close to the cricket ground,' put in John with a laugh, then, as an afterthought, he added, 'You will join the team, old man, won't you?'

'I dare say I will.' Stephen grinned at John's suddenly anxious expression. 'Although goodness knows when I'm going to find the time for all these activities.'

'Surely things are easier now at the surgery?' Amanda commented as she helped herself to some fruit. 'Now that you have your new clinics. Oh, and not forgetting your new nurse, of course.' She grinned at Helen.

'Yes, things are easier,' Stephen agreed. 'But a GP's lot is still a hectic one.'

'My heart bleeds for you,' laughed John. 'You should try caring for people's souls for a while and see how difficult that is!' He leaned forward and cut himself a wedge of Brie, then, turning to Helen, he said, 'And how is it all working out for you, Helen?'

She hesitated. 'Well, it's very different

from what I was doing before, but I was prepared for that. As the daughter of a rural GP I had a rough idea about general practice and wasn't under any illusions, but having said that,' she glanced round the table at the others, 'I must admit to having been pleasantly surprised. I thought I'd miss hospital life, the city and the fast pace, but I haven't—not one bit.' She paused as if the fact surprised even herself.

'So you will be staying?' asked John.

'I don't know—it depends on many things. I only took the job at the surgery on a month's trial, to see if it suited me and equally to see if I fitted in.'

'What about your fiancé?' remarked Stephen suddenly. 'I shouldn't think he'd be too happy if you stayed. After all, the Island isn't the easiest of places to get to in a hurry.'

For a moment the silence was almost deafening, and it was Amanda who finally broke it. 'Oh, Helen's not engaged.' She glanced up at Stephen from under her black lashes, then across the table to Helen, 'Are you, Helen?' she finished.

Coolly Stephen transferred his gaze from Helen to Amanda and back to Helen. 'I'm sorry,' he apologised, 'Perhaps I should have said your boyfriend.'

'You mean the registrar?' Amanda prattled on, ignoring her husband's warning glance. 'Oh, but that's all over. Helen told me so when she first arrived, didn't you, Helen?' She turned to Helen, then, seeing her expression and sensing the sudden tension in the atmosphere, she clapped a hand over her mouth. 'Oh, dear! What have I said? Oh, John, I've done it again!' She threw her husband an appealing look, but the wicked gleam still shone in her eyes and Helen knew she had fully intended to say what she had.

Helen stared at the table, unable to meet Stephen's gaze. However was she going to explain why she had deliberately misled him? She was saved for the time being, however, as John, who seemed more than used to dealing with his wife's *faux pas*, cleverly changed the subject.

As Amanda stood up to make the coffee her husband asked Stephen if he would like to see the new computer in his study, and the two men disappeared, leaving the girls alone.

As soon as the kitchen door closed behind the men, Amanda turned from the Aga and looked at Helen.

'Are you very cross with me?'

Helen shrugged and began pleating the hem of her serviette. She was annoyed with Amanda because she felt that somehow she had engineered what had happened, but she didn't feel she could make a fuss about it, especially after Amanda's hospitality.

'You didn't want Stephen to know you'd split up with your boyfriend, did you?'

Helen shook her head, suddenly at a loss for words.

'But why?' Amanda frowned. 'I don't understand.'

'I don't really know—I suppose I felt it would complicate our relationship,' said Helen slowly, then, as Amanda raised her eyebrows, she added hastily, 'Our working relationship, that is.'

Amanda didn't answer immediately, busying herself with plugging in the percolator, then she said, 'He's very fond of you, you know.'

'Who, Stephen?' Helen gave a nervous laugh. 'Don't be silly, you're imagining things.'

'Oh, no, I'm not. I've seen the way he looks at you.'

'Well, you're mistaken—and I have it on

very good authority that he's a confirmed bachelor.'

'All men are confirmed bachelors until they fall in love,' Amanda quipped lightly.

'Now you really are being ridiculous,' retorted Helen, but she was forced to laugh. Then, falling serious again, she added, 'I'm just not interested, Amanda, you must understand that. I'm not ready for another relationship, in fact I sometimes wonder whether I'll trust anyone ever again after Giles...'

'Giles? Was that his name?'

'Yes.'

'So what did he do to make you distrust men so much?'

'He was married.'

'And you didn't know?'

Helen shook her head.

'Oh, a real rat...well, I'm sure Stephen's not like that. He's a great guy—everyone adores him. He's wonderful with kids —why, you've seen how he is with Katy...'

'Yes, and he's also self-opinionated over his work and he wants all his own way and won't rest until he gets it,' Helen replied heatedly.

Amanda stared at her, then shrugged. 'Well, I suppose no one's perfect, but I think you'd go a long way to find another one like Stephen—with the exception of John, of course.' She suddenly smiled. 'And you can't have him, because he's mine.' Then she added, 'What do you think of him?'

'John? He's a lovely man—I can quite see why you fell for him.' Helen's face softened.

'I never believed in love at first sight until I met John,' said Amanda dreamily as she set out the coffee-cups.

'How did you meet him?' Helen was curious, wondering how the paths of a vicar and a potential film star had crossed.

'It was when I was still at drama school. He officiated at a friend's wedding—she introduced us, and that was that.'

'But what about your career?'

'At first I intended to continue with it—literally with John's blessing—then Katy was born, and after her condition was diagnosed, I really had no further choice. She's my career now.' A shadowed look had come into Amanda's dark eyes as she spoke of her daughter.

'That must have been a huge sacrifice,' said Helen, remembering how desperate Amanda had been to act.

Her friend shrugged. 'Not really. The biggest sacrifice is that we've decided not to risk having any more children.'

They were silent for a moment, then Helen said, 'I'm sorry, Amanda, I really am, but about Katy—you mustn't ever give up hope you know—with modern research anything is possible.'

Before Amanda had a chance to reply, the men returned and she suggested they took their coffee into the sitting-room, where for the next hour they sat in front of the hearth enjoying the warmth of a blazing log fire.

CHAPTER NINE

It was nearly midnight before they left, and as they made their farewells Helen felt her apprehension mounting. Surely, during the walk home, Stephen would ask why she had deliberately misled him over Giles? The problem was she didn't really know herself, so how could she hope to explain it to him? Deep down she knew that Stephen wasn't a womaniser and that he hadn't attempted to take advantage of either her or the situation. The one kiss they had shared had been completely spontaneous, a mutual experience, totally unpremeditated. To add to her confusion, since dinner Stephen had been very quiet, and as they moved into the hall with their hosts, Helen found herself dreading the forthcoming confrontation.

They stepped outside to a heavy drizzle, but as they started off down the path John called after them. 'Hold on a minute, you'll get soaked walking home in this. Here, borrow my umbrella.' He reached behind the door and produced a large black clerical umbrella.

Stephen smiled. 'Thanks, John, we'll return it tomorrow,' he said as he struggled with the clasp.

Helen looked back, and was just in time to see John slip an arm around Amanda's shoulders before they disappeared inside.

Large as the umbrella was, they had to walk very close together, and Helen was deeply aware of Stephen's body against hers as they walked through the silent village. The dreaded question, however, didn't come, and apart from a few comments about Katy they remained quiet.

In spite of her relief Helen was uncomfortably aware of a growing sense of unease which mingled with a sudden overwhelming desire for him to take her into her arms again. She had no explanation for her feelings, maybe she had simply drunk too much of John's barley wine, but whatever it was she knew she suddenly wanted to set the record straight between herself and Stephen. The matter had become urgent and she couldn't bear to think that her thoughtless deceit might have hurt him.

By the time she had marshalled her confused thoughts into some sort of order they had reached the house, and Stephen ushered her into the porch and closed the umbrella, shaking the water from it as he did so.

When he turned he seemed surprised that she was still in the porch and hadn't gone indoors. Their eyes met and in a purely involuntary gesture Helen reached out and touched his arm.

'Stephen.' She swallowed, uncertain how to proceed. 'Stephen, I believe I owe you an apology and an explanation.' She could see his features quite clearly in the hall light which shone through the stained glass panel above the door.

He raised his eyebrows. 'Your personal life is entirely your own affair. It really has nothing to do with me.'

'But...but I led you to believe...'

'Whatever you wanted me to believe is your business—it has nothing whatever to do with me. I'm simply your employer.'

She stared at him in dismay. There was a bleakness about him that she had never seen before, and in that instant she knew without doubt that she had indeed hurt him when she had deliberately led him to believe she was deeply committed elsewhere.

There was something about his approach and his reactions that she found old-fashioned. She couldn't for one moment imagine Giles behaving in the same way, given the same set of circumstances, for he was an opportunist and would take advantage of any situation. Then briefly she recalled Mrs Parkes telling her that Stephen was a gentleman, something rarely found in these days of liberated equality. Even as she battled to find the right words to banish that look from his face, they heard the sound of a car followed by the flash of headlights in the drive, then

Oliver's Land Rover crunched to a halt in front of the porch.

They waited as he climbed down, and Helen was struck by the air of weariness about him.

'I hope,' said Stephen, 'that wasn't one of my patients you've been visiting at this time of night.'

The older man shook his head. 'No, it was a home confinement up on the new estate. Nice little family, second baby, all doing well.'

They followed him into the house, and he paused in the hallway, taking off his hat and hanging it on the stand, then opening his surgery door he dumped his bag on the desk. Turning to Stephen and Helen, he said, 'If you two will excuse me, I'm off to bed. Help yourselves to a nightcap. Goodnight.' He waved his hand and began to climb the stairs.

'Goodnight, Dad.' Helen stood in the hall and watched him anxiously, then just as she was about to turn away, Oliver stopped.

'Oh, I almost forgot,' he said, looking down at them. 'The hospital phoned just after you'd gone out—Walt Foster died this evening. Apparently he arrested again, a massive one, nothing they could do this time.'

By the time he had finished speaking he had turned on to the landing, so it was Stephen who saw Helen's stricken expression.

Without a word he took her arm and led her into the sitting-room. The last embers of the fire were still glowing, and as Helen shivered Stephen threw another log on the fire, then sitting down on the sofa he reached up, took her hand and drew her down beside him.

'He seemed so well this morning,' she said, staring unseeingly into the fire as Stephen leaned forward, picked up the poker and coaxed the embers into life. 'I really thought he was going to pull through,' she added quietly.

'You know how quickly these things can change,' he said gently. They were silent for a moment watching tiny tongues of flame licking the pine log that Walt had felled.

'I'm glad I went to see him.' A lump had risen in Helen's throat and she felt suddenly overwhelmed. Tears filled her eyes and she wasn't sure if they were for Walt Foster, little Katy Foxe or for herself and her shattered dreams.

'Life can be a real bitch sometimes, can't it?' Stephen glanced at her as if he were reading her thoughts, then he slid one arm along the back of the sofa behind her.

She nodded and swallowed, her eyes still bright.

'Want to talk about it?' His tone was deliberately casual.

She threw him a startled glance. Only minutes ago he had told her that her private life was her own business, now it seemed he was offering to listen.

'It might help—a trouble shared and all that,' he said as he saw her look, then when still she hesitated, he said unexpectedly, 'Are you still in love with him?'

'No...yes...I don't know...' Helen's voice sank to a whisper.

'So what went wrong? You said he was a registrar? On the same unit as you?' When she nodded, he commented, 'Ideal set-up, I would have thought, so what was the fly in the ointment?'

'He was married.'

'I see.' Stephen's reply was non-committal, then glancing at the sideboard, he said, 'How about that nightcap?' She nodded, and he stood up and crossed the room. 'Brandy?'

'Yes, please.' She watched him as he poured the drinks, the firelight playing on his strong features and accentuating the glints in his hair, then as he returned to her side and handed her her drink his fingers touched hers. She didn't immediately withdraw her hand, and as she raised her eyes to his she saw a look of such compassion that her tears threatened to flow.

He took his seat beside her, but this time he sat closer, his thigh brushing hers. 'Now where were we? Ah, yes, you'd just told me that your registrar was married. I take it he hadn't chosen to give you that choice little bit of information before?'

She shook her head, sipped her brandy before carefully setting down her glass on the coffee-table, then took a deep breath and it all came tumbling out. She told him how she had met Giles and fallen for him immediately, about his wealthy background, how he had wined and dined her, introducing her to another, more sophisticated world, how he had appeared to return her love, but then how had come the final shattering betrayal.

Stephen remained silent all the while she was talking, and when she had finished, her anger and passion spent, and the tears on her cheeks glistening in the firelight, he turned and gathered her into his arms.

With a sigh Helen leaned against him. Drained now of all emotion after the physical effort of recounting her story, she was content to simply relax, her head on his shoulder. She felt a sense of peace, as if she had been battling blindly through a wilderness but had finally found sanctuary.

She didn't know how long she lay in the circle of Stephen's arms with the only sounds in the room the beating of their hearts and the occasional crackling of the pine log as it burnt, spluttered and finally fell apart. And all the while Stephen gently stroked her hair, never once uttering one word of either reproach or advice.

Then, as the clock in the hall chimed two, he stirred and, looking down at her, he gently cupped her chin, lifting her face to his. With the merest touch his lips brushed her forehead, then her cheeks, her eyelids, and finally covered her mouth in a kiss so light she wondered if she had imagined it. A tingle fluttered the length of her spine and, when she neither resisted nor uttered a word of protest, he held her face between both hands, his strong fingers moving and caressing, becoming entangled in her hair as his mouth finally claimed hers.

Helen had no idea when it was that her mood changed, but somewhere she slipped from simply needing Stephen's comfort and reassurance into wanting him with a surge of desire that suddenly flared deep inside her. At the same time she became aware that Stephen's role had changed dramatically from confidant and friend to that of a lover with a need and desire every bit as urgent as her own.

Her mouth opened beneath his and as his hands moved, roaming urgently over her body, she was shaken by the intensity of her response. She had only known such passion with one other man, and she would never have believed it possible that she could be feeling that way again. Or could it be simply that it was still Giles she loved and yearned for and Stephen was simply a substitute?

As these disquieting thoughts flitted through her brain she drew back from Stephen, and he, sensing her sudden withdrawal, moved away from her. Taking a deep breath, he visibly fought to control himself.

For a long moment they stared at each other, then Stephen, in a gesture of helplessness, ran his fingers through his hair.

'Oh, God, Helen, I'm sorry. I didn't mean that to happen.' Helplessly he turned his face away, staring into the fire.

Leaning forward, Helen touched his arm and, startled, he looked back at her.

'It's all right, Stephen. Really...I was as much to blame.'

'You mean...?' He stared at her as if he hardly dared to hope that she not only wasn't annoyed with him but that she might have actually enjoyed what had happened.

She sighed. 'I don't know, Stephen—I just don't know. It's too soon. I think I need some time to sort myself out.'

'Well, I'm not going anywhere.' Gently he stroked the back of his fingers down the side of her cheek, just as he had done once before when they had been sitting in his car.

This time, however, the gesture caused another delicious tingle to Helen's spine and lifting her eyes to his, she said softly,

'What are you saying?'

'Simply that I want you to take all the time you need, and I intend to stick around until you do.' With that he stood up, and looking down at her with an expression in his hazel eyes that seemed to turn her knees to water, he held out his hand. 'Now I think you'd better get yourself to bed—it's been quite a day.'

His hand gripped hers, he helped her to her feet and for a moment she leaned against him, resting her head against his chest, then, standing on tiptoe, she kissed his cheek.

'Thank you, Stephen,' she whispered, then, not trusting her tattered emotions a moment longer, she hurried from the room.

In spite of her fatigue, sleep did not come easily to Helen as her troubled thoughts chased themselves round in her head. She had no explanation for what had happened between herself and Stephen, and after much soul-searching she could only come to the conclusion that in her desperation for a scrap of comfort she had mistaken her feelings for passion. But that gave no explanation for Stephen's reactions, and those she found almost as difficult to accept as her own. Her father had told her that Stephen was a confirmed bachelor, implying that he wasn't interested in long-term relationships, then Amanda had stated that it was perfectly obvious that Stephen was fond of her, Helen, and these facts only left her feeling more confused than ever.

Helen had never been one to love lightly, and for her, her commitment to Giles had been total; surely therefore the intense feelings she had experienced with Stephen had been false?

Well into the small hours her troubled thoughts chased each other, and it was nearly dawn before she fell into an uneasy sleep; when later she appeared at breakfast, pale and drawn, it attracted even her father's attention.

'Are we working you too hard, Helen?' he asked as he unfolded his copy of the *Guardian*.

She smiled and shook her head, saying that she'd simply had a bad night, only too conscious as she spoke of Stephen's concerned look.

Saturday mornings followed a different procedure, with only an emergency surgery being held and each doctor taking it in turns to be on duty for the entire weekend. Once the surgery was over Helen's weekend was her own, but she found herself restlessly wandering the house, unable to settle to anything. It was Stephen's weekend on call, and it was proving to be a busy one, with one visit after another.

Helen finally took herself off with Plummer to visit Katy and to return John's umbrella.

When she arrived at the Vicarage it was to find Amanda engaged in Katy's physiotherapy session. The little girl was lying face down across the arm of an easy chair while her mother administered the special massage that was necessary to keep her lungs clear.

'How long do you do this for?' asked Helen as she sat down.

'At least two hours a day,' replied Amanda.

'You must find it exhausting,' Helen remarked, admiring her friend's devotion.

'Not really. It just has to be done. It's part of our daily routine now. John helps, of course, when he's here, and some of the church ladies come in and take a turn. They've formed a rota to help me with

Katy in various ways. I don't know how I'd manage without them.'

'I'd like to help when I can,' said Helen spontaneously, 'so stick my name on the rota.'

Amanda paused and looked up. 'Does that mean you've decided to stay?'

'Not exactly,' said Helen, then added swiftly, 'But I'm here for the time being, so let's just take each day as it comes. What a marvellous view you have from here.' Deliberately she changed the subject, lifting her head and looking out of the tall windows which looked down the valley to the creek.

'Yes, it is lovely, isn't it?' Amanda agreed, then added, 'In summer it's wonderful, and on a clear day you can see right across the marshes. Talking of the marshes, do you think Stephen will go and look at Heron Cottage?'

Helen shrugged. 'I expect so; he said he would.'

'Why do you think he wants his own place?' Amanda gave her a sly look from under her lashes, and to her annoyance Helen felt her cheeks grow hot.

'He never intended to remain at High Pines. He said it was only temporary until he found a place of his own.'

'Maybe he's thinking of settling down.' Amanda tried to sound nonchalant, but as she stood up, she caught Helen's eye and suddenly both girls laughed.

'You really are the limit, Amanda,' scolded Helen. 'I know exactly what you're thinking, but you're wrong.'

'I wouldn't bet on it,' Amanda replied darkly. 'I told you last night that I reckon he's fond of you, and, the more I think about it, the more convinced I am.'

'Well, I'm sorry to disappoint you, but it takes two for what you have in mind and, as I've already told you, I'm just not interested.'

Amanda shrugged, went to put the kettle on and seemed prepared for the moment to let the matter drop, but later, as Helen walked home, she knew she had lied to her friend, for in spite of all her earlier resolutions, she had been quite unable to get Stephen out of her mind since the previous evening.

It was the same for the remainder of the weekend, and, although she saw very little of Stephen she felt restless, and hardly a moment passed when she didn't think of him. In the end she was quite relieved when Monday morning arrived and she could become involved in her work again.

Helen's first job of the morning was to open the post, sort, stamp and date each letter, and divide them into two trays—one for each of the doctors. While she was doing this she was constantly answering the telephone, arranging appointments and making notes of any house calls for later in the day.

While the doctors were reading their post she would sort the patients' records for the morning surgeries and prepare her treatment-room. Finally she would collect the post from the doctors' rooms and file any hospital letters, laboratory test results or discharge summaries in the appropriate patient's records.

On that particular morning as she picked up her father's tray he looked up, peering over the top of his spectacles. 'There's a letter there from David Blake,' he said, referring to the general surgeon at the hospital. 'He's performed a biopsy on Mrs Prescott. We'll just have to wait for the results now.'

Helen nodded, then had to hurry back to her desk to answer the telephone. She was pleased that things had moved so swiftly for Lily Prescott, but she knew that the worry wouldn't be over until the tests had been done to see whether or not the lump was malignant or a harmless benign tumour.

As the last days of autumn passed Helen became more and more involved in her work. The last lingering leaves fell from the trees in the orchard and a chill crept into the air along with several overnight frosts. The days shortened and the folk in the village began to talk about Christmas. Helen's trial month at the surgery was almost up, and still she was no nearer knowing what she was going to do.

Her father and Mrs Parkes wanted her to stay, that went without saying, for while Oliver didn't want to stand in the way of her career he also couldn't hide his pleasure at having her living at home again. The patients also seemed to have taken her to their hearts, but for Helen herself, doubts still lingered. As for Stephen Brett, what he wanted still remained a mystery. He seemed to have accepted her on a professional basis, but since the evening they had spent together, when she had opened her heart to him, and he had given her a glimpse of his own feelings, indicating that he wanted more to come of their relationship, he had behaved impeccably.

In fact on several occasions Helen found herself wondering if she had dreamed the whole thing. He now acted in a friendly, almost brotherly way towards her when they weren't working, and when they were his attitude was correct and purely professional. He made no further attempt to touch her, and as the days passed she began to find the situation unnerving.

In the surgery the newly formed clinics ran smoothly, and during one of Helen's cervical smear clinics Maureen Arnold arrived for her appointment. Helen was concerned to see that the woman looked more tense and anxious than she had when she had treated her for her cut finger.

As she prepared her for her smear Helen talked in a calm, almost chatty fashion, hoping she would persuade her to relax. She had a feeling here was something worrying Maureen and she hoped she might unburden herself.

'How's the family?' Helen asked as she

prepared the speculum and pulled on her surgical gloves.

'All right, I suppose,' Maureen replied dully.

'How old are the children now?' Helen knew perfectly well, having seen both of them in the course of her work, but she pretended she'd forgotten.

'Scott's ten and Beverley's eight.'

'So Beverley still goes to the village school?'

'Yes. Scott's at the middle school in Newport.' Maureen's attitude softened slightly as she spoke of her children, and Helen, sensing the slight relaxing of tension, quickly and expertly took her smear.

As she applied the fixative to the glass slide for testing at the laboratory she said casually, 'And your husband? How is he?'

Maureen didn't answer immediately, and Helen instinctively knew she had touched on the problem area. By this time Maureen was sitting on the side of the examination couch, then as Helen glanced enquiringly at her, she shrugged.

'He's all right, I suppose.' She hesitated, then under her breath, she added, 'In the circumstances.'

'And what circumstances are those?' Helen tried to keep her tone light so that it wouldn't sound as if she were prying.

'He's been made redundant—from his factory job.'

'Oh, dear,' Helen looked up. 'I'm sorry to hear that.' She noticed that Maureen was chewing at her lower lip in agitation.

'Don't know what we're going to do—the job sounded so good—we came here from the mainland, got ourselves a mortgage, now God knows how we're going to pay it!'

As Helen listened she remembered Maureen previously telling her that they lived in one of the new houses on the estate.

'Try not to worry too much,' she said gently. 'Something will turn up, you'll see.'

Maureen shrugged again and pulled on her coat. 'And if it doesn't, who pays the bills?'

'You can get help, you know.'

'We don't want charity,' Maureen replied stiffly, tightening the belt of her coat.

'It isn't charity, Maureen,' Helen turned and looked at her sharply. 'It's your right to seek help when times are hard.'

'Yes, well, let's hope it won't come to that. Thank you, Nurse—goodbye.' With her head high Maureen walked quickly from the surgery.

Helen watched her walk down the path, then, shaking her head, she went to call her next patient.

The following day Amanda brought Katy to the surgery on their way home from the play-group to collect a repeat prescription. When the little girl saw Helen she waved excitedly.

'She's got something to tell you.' Amanda smiled.

'Going to be an angel,' said Katy proudly.

'An angel? But that's wonderful!' Helen crouched down beside the little girl. 'When is this going to be? At Christmas?'

Katy shook her head and glanced up at her mother.

'It's her play-group,' Amanda explained. 'John's letting them do their Nativity play in the church just before Christmas and they've asked Katy to be an angel. She's so excited, she couldn't wait to tell someone. She wants you and Stephen to come and watch her.'

'And Plummer,' interrupted Katy.

Helen laughed. 'Well, I shall certainly be there if I can, but I don't know about Plummer.' She looked at Amanda and added, 'I've heard of them using a real donkey at Nativities, but I'm not so sure they'd want a delinquent spaniel.'

After saying goodbye to Amanda and Katy, she went back into the treatment-room where she was to assist Stephen in the removal of a papilloma from an elderly man's neck. After preparing her treatment trolley she called the patient, assisted him on to the couch and told him to make himself comfortable. At that moment Stephen entered the room, and as his eyes mets hers her heart skipped a beat. This wasn't the first time this had happened, for just lately Helen had found she was aware of him practically every moment of the day.

He, however, seemed as casual as ever, as if he were totally unaware of her reaction to his nearness. 'Did I hear Katy's voice?' he asked after he had greeted the patient and was busy scrubbing up at the sink.

'Yes, they've just left.' Helen went on to tell him about the Nativity play and how the little girl wanted them both to go.

He looked thoughtful. 'Hmm—Christmas,

you say? Well, I shall certainly be able to go, but what about you?'

She looked up, startled. 'What do you mean?'

'Will you still be here at Christmas?'

Their eyes met again across the examination couch, a flush touching Helen's cheeks as she read the meaning in Stephen's question, and the elderly patient, in sudden interest, looked from one to the other.

'I don't know,' she replied at last. Then she busied herself with adjusting the light above the couch and swabbing the area of skin on the patient's neck with Hibitane solution. She tried to avoid meeting Stephen's gaze again, and even when he asked her to draw up five mls of Xylocaine for the local anaesthetic she wouldn't meet his eyes.

Stephen administered the injection and, while they waited for it to take effect, he chattered to the patient to relax him. Finally, at a sign from Stephen, Helen tested the patient's reaction with with tip of a sterile needle. When there was no response Stephen picked up the cautery from the trolley, switched it on and expertly removed the papilloma.

Afterwards Helen blotted up the few

drops of blood, applying pressure to the tiny wound with a gauze swab, then carefully, after Stephen had checked it and given a few words of reassurance to the patient, she applied a sterile dressing.

As she was clearing up after the patient had left she was suddenly conscious that Stephen was very quiet. She threw him a glance and saw that he was fiddling with some instruments on the trolley. There was a frown on his face and Helen got the impression that he wanted to say something but didn't know how to begin.

At last as she was almost out of the door he cleared his throat. 'Helen, just a minute.'

She paused and came back into the room, waiting for him to continue. Outwardly she appeared calm, but inwardly she felt tension gathering.

'Are you doing anything between now and evening surgery?' he asked.

'No, I don't think so. Why?'

'Well, a few days ago I went to see Heron Cottage. I liked it and I'm considering making an offer. I wondered if you'd come and have a look at it and see what you think.'

She raised her eyebrows, trying desperately to appear calm, but her heart was pounding. 'Why me?' she queried.

'I just thought it would be nice to have a second opinion.' He tried to match his tone to hers for casualness, she knew he was as on edge as she was.

'All right.' She shrugged lightly. 'Just give me ten minutes to change.'

As she ran upstairs her senses were reeling. Why should Stephen have asked her to give her opinion on his future home? What possible difference could it make to him whether she liked it or not?

CHAPTER TEN

Heron Cottage, situated at the far end of Vicarage Lane, overlooked the creek and a vast area of marshland renowned by the locals for its natural beauty and wildlife.

While Stephen was parking the car in a little lay-by further up the lane Helen walked back to the cottage, staring up at it with interest. She could see that it had changed very little since her childhood.

Although called a cottage, in reality Heron Cottage was a house with roughcast walls whitewashed beneath a slated roof, its bedroom windows tucked away under the eaves. A creeping ivy covered a large portion of the exterior, curling around the Georgian-style windows and above the storm porch.

'Do you know the man who lived here?' asked Stephen as he caught up with her and unlatched the gate, its once white paint all but disappeared with the effects of time and weather.

'Sam Bartholomew?' Helen reflected for a moment. 'I can't say I know him personally, but he's such a character around here that everyone feels they know him. He was a great seafaring man, a professional yachtsman in fact, until he retired. He'll be greatly missed in the village. I hope he'll be able to settle in his new home.'

'I should think he would,' Stephen replied as they walked up the path between flowerbeds, well cared for once but overgrown now with banks of hydrangeas, their flower heads transparent and devoid of colour. 'Oliver was telling me that the home Sam's going to overlooks the Solent, so he'll be able to watch all the Cowes Week activities.'

As Stephen fiddled with a bunch of keys Helen looked back at the forlorn garden where thick wodges of dead leaves, damp and almost black, choked the flower borders and the only splashes of colour came from clumps of Michaelmas daisies and the odd brave rose that lingered, defying the night frost.

The black studded oak door swung open as Stephen pushed it and stood back, allowing Helen to cross the threshold ahead of him.

Immediately they were enveloped by the atmosphere of Heron Cottage. It was still partly furnished, for Sam had only taken his personal possessions and a few smaller items of furniture. The highly polished parquet floors were scattered with rag rugs and deep, comfortable-looking chintz-covered chairs and sofas dotted the living area. Several watercolours, all with a marine theme, adorned the walls together with one or two Brannon-style prints of old Island scenes. Stephen glanced at the brochure that the agents had given him and commented that everything left was to be sold with the property.

The rooms were low-ceilinged and seemed to sprawl into each other, with archways where one might have expected doors and unusual exciting features like an inglenook fireplace, window seats and a twisted wooden staircase in the corner of the sitting-room. The kitchen had a flagstoned floor, an old-fashioned range to cook by and an adjoining pantry.

Helen exclaimed with delight as she moved swiftly from room to room, examining everything on the ground floor and then, with Stephen close behind, climbing the stairs to explore the bedrooms and the funny little attic-type rooms that nestled in the roof.

Leaning her hands on the sill in one of these tiny rooms, she looked out across the marshes where the late afternoon mist was beginning to descend, curling wraith-like between vast clumps of reeds.

'Oh, Stephen, it's absolutely enchanting!' she breathed. 'I came here with my mother, a long time ago, but I'd quite forgotten how beautiful it was.'

'You like it?' Although there was a smile on his face there was a note of anxiety in his voice, as if it meant a great deal to him that she should like this cottage.

'It's perfect!'

'The agents say it has great potential.'

'What do they mean by that?' Helen turned from the window in alarm.

Stephen shrugged. 'I don't know—I suppose they mean that bits could be pulled down and other bits built on. There are probably a hundred and one things that could be done to modernise it.'

'Oh, but you wouldn't! You couldn't...it would spoil it,' Helen shuddered. 'It would quite lose its charm, with extensions and patio windows and all the other dreadful things they do to old houses these days.'

He smiled. 'You know, really you're quite an old-fashioned girl under that city-type image, aren't you?'

'Am I?' She looked surprised, then smiled. 'Yes, I suppose I am. It must be to do with my traditional upbringing.'

'It could be that,' he mused. 'Or on the other hand, it could be that you were simply saying the opposite to me.' When she raised her eyebrows in surprise he continued, 'You thought I might be going to modernise this place, so you protested—if I'd said I was going to leave it as it was, you would probably have said it needed updating.'

'Stephen!' She sounded shocked. 'How could you say such a thing? Why sould I say something just to be the opposite to you?' As she spoke he moved towards her and she, seeing the look in his eyes, turned back to the window in sudden confusion.

'Because,' he said softly, 'it seems to me that you're taking great delight in teasing me and driving me wild.'

Helen stiffened as she felt his arms go round her and his warm breath on the nape of her neck. Sharply she lifted her head just as he lowered his, and as his arms tightened she felt his lips touch the hollow between her neck and shoulder. Helplessly she leaned against him, becoming aware of the tautening of his own body in response to hers.

'I wasn't aware I was doing that,' she murmured. 'And I've certainly never before been accused of being a tease.'

He groaned, a low throaty sound that sent a thrill shooting through her. 'No, I doubt whether you have been aware of what you've been doing to me. And it's probably a blessing that you haven't. It could have been decidedly embarrassing in the treatment-room if you'd been aware of the devastating effect you were having upon me. Oh, Helen,' once again he groaned, 'I know I said I was prepared to wait while you sorted yourself out, but there are limits to how much a man can take.'

'So what do you want me to do about it?' she whispered.

'Well, couldn't you make the waiting a bit more exciting?' As he spoke he turned her to face him. 'Not, of course, that the way you look doesn't excite me,' he added, taking in her neat figure in her close-fitting jeans and sweater and her long blonde hair which this afternoon she had tied back into a pony-tail. 'But a little more excitement wouldn't come amiss.'

Lifting her head, Helen looked up into his eyes, and as his hands encircled her waist she ran her own hands up his arms, across his shoulders, linking them at the back of his neck and allowing her fingers to become entangled in his hair. Then gently she coaxed his head down until his mouth was only inches from her own.

'Is this what you mean?' she murmured, then her lips parted, yielding to his mouth which possessed hers in sudden urgent passion.

Fiercely he pulled her close, almost crushing her against his chest, and as a shaft of desire coursed through her and she strained her body against his she knew his need was as great as hers. For an unknown space of time Helen was oblivious to all but the passion that consumed them both, and as she returned his kisses, welcoming and wanting every advance he made, she knew that it would be very easy to surrender to him totally.

Then when they were very close to that treacherous moment of no return, sanity momentarily returned and reluctantly she pulled away, turning from him as they both struggled to regain control of their emotions. Shakily she pushed back several strands of hair that had come loose. Once again the intensity of her response to this man's desire had shocked her, and this time she was left in no doubt that all the feeling had been for him, Stephen, and not for some substitute for Giles.

It troubled her, however, that this could have happened so quickly, and she worried that it could be on the rebound. Stephen must have caught her troubled look, for gently he leaned towards her and traced a line down the soft skin of her cheek.

'What is it, Helen? Am I rushing you again?'

She sighed. 'I'm sorry, Stephen, truly I am, and please believe me when I say I'm not a tease. It's just that I can't believe what's happening to me...to us.'

'Why not believe it? Why not just accept it?'

'I only wish I could...but it's just that it's too soon. You see, I loved Giles totally, Stephen—I trusted him implicity, and he betrayed that trust. I would never in a million years have believed that I could feel like that again about someone, and so soon. I'm frightened, Stephen. I'm frightened to love again.'

'My poor little love,' he murmured, once again drawing her into his arms. 'That bastard Patterson really loused things up for you, didn't he? Well, Helen, I'm not like him. For a start, I'm not married and never have been. I won't deny there've been other women—one in particular was pretty special, but it wasn't meant to be. I don't love lightly or casually, but when I do I mean it. Helen, are you listening to me?' He tilted her chin, forcing her to look into his eyes. 'I told you before I was prepared to wait, and I still am—just so long as in the end you give me the answer I want to hear. You've done something to me, Helen. I'm not sure what it is, but from the moment you chucked that cup of coffee over me I haven't been able to get you out of my mind. I want you and I'm prepared to wait, but in the meantime do you think you could at least tell me you like me a bit, just so I've got something to be going on with?'

In spite of the intensity of her emotions Helen found herself laughing. 'Oh, Stephen, I don't just like you a bit—I like you a lot. You must know that. What's been happening between us has knocked me sideways.' Reaching up, she twined her arms around his neck again. 'In fact, I think I could go so far as to say that for the past couple of weeks I've been truly happy.'

'Does that mean, Sister Meredith,' Stephen grew serious, 'that you might just consider staying on at the surgery for a while longer?' A gleam came into his eyes as he looked down at her and he brought his hands to rest lightly on her hips.

'It's funny you should ask that, because I believe it was a certain Dr Brett who didn't want me there in the first place.'

He grinned. 'If, just this once, I was to confess to having been wrong, would you reconsider and stay on—at least until after Christmas? That way you'll keep everyone happy; Oliver who couldn't bear it if you disappeared again now, Mrs Parkes who, if you've noticed recently, has a certain look in her eye whenever she sees us together, Katy whom you've promised to watch in her Nativity play, and, last but by no means least, me, because I can't bear to let you out of my sight for more than five minutes. And who knows, by the time Christmas is over, you might...just might have had time to sort yourself out and decide that you'd like to come and live with me here in Heron Cottage!'

He took a deep breath while Helen, helpless with laughter at his tirade, stood on tiptoe and planted a kiss on his mouth. When she would have pulled away, however, he tightened his hold, imprisoning her against the window-frame while his mouth claimed hers again in a kiss that told her he had meant every word.

At last, when she finally managed to disentangle herself, Helen looked at her watch. 'Stephen, do you realise what time it is? If we're going to be in time for evening surgery we'll have to go now.'

He sighed reluctantly and followed her down the stairs, ducking his head beneath a particularly low beam.

After he had locked the door they got into the car and, with a last lingering look at Heron Cottage, they drew away up Vicarage Lane.

Helen glanced at Stephen, and although his profile was only just discernible in the gathering dusk he appeared happy and relaxed. With a little sigh she leaned her head back, trying to recall the things he had said, then, as she remembered that he had told her that there had once been someone else who had been very special, a pang shot through her that could only be jealousy. She recalled what her father had said about him.

He turned his head, and taking one hand from the steering wheel reached out, covering her hand where it lay in her lap.

'Penny for your thoughts?'

There was a teasing note in his voice, but for a moment Helen hesitated, almost afraid to tell him what she'd been thinking, then when he prompted her by squeezing her hand, she said slowly, 'I was just wondering about the rumour I'd heard about you.'

'Rumour?' He turned his head again and the surprise registered in his tone.

'Yes, I was told that you were a confirmed bachelor.'

He threw back his head and laughed aloud.

'So it isn't true, then?' She shot him a quick glance.

'Not true? Of course it is—I like my freedom.'

'Oh! But I thought...just now, back there...I thought...' she trailed off in confusion.

'You thought when I said I wanted you to come and live with me at Heron Cottage that I meant I wanted you to marry me?'

The teasing note was still in his voice, but for a moment Helen wasn't sure whether he was serious or not and she was glad of the dusk which covered her embarrassment. Obviously she had misunderstood him, for what she had taken as a proposal had been nothing of the sort. But there was no way she wanted to enter into another relationship like the one she'd had with Giles.

When she didn't answer, he leaned forward slightly, taking his eyes from the road for a second, trying to look at her, then seriously he said, 'Helen, my love, I'm sorry. I was teasing—you were quite right, I do want you to marry me. I wouldn't want it any other way. If we move into Heron Cottage, it'll be as man and wife. I'm a pretty conventional sort of guy, you know.' He chuckled and she found herself smiling. He was so easy to be with, and she was discovering a humorous side to his nature that appealed to her.

They pulled out of Vicarage Lane and into the main village street. Lights were shining in the cottages around the green, and as they passed the Post Office they saw Lily Prescott standing in the doorway about to pull down her shop blinds. She peered into the car as they passed, then waved for them to stop.

Stephen pulled into the kerb and Helen wound down her window. 'Hello, Mrs Prescott, how are you?' she said.

'Hello, Helen, love,' she leaned forward so that she could see Stephen. 'Good evening, Dr Brett. Helen, I've just had a visit from Dr Meredith.'

'Have you?' said Helen in surprise. 'Is anything wrong?'

'No, love. Everything's fine—he came to tell me he'd had a letter from the hospital to say I'm in the clear. I was that surprised to see him, because I've got an appointment with you tomorrow to have my stitches out. I thought I'd wait until then to get my results.'

'Oh, I'm so pleased, Mrs Prescott,' Helen smiled.

'You see, that old lump wasn't anything to worry about after all.' She laughed, but Helen could see the lines of tension on her face. 'Well, I must be going, dear, I'm going to have a little celebration drink with my sister. See you tomorrow.' She turned away, then paused and looked back towards the car, a curious expression on her face. 'Been up to the Vicarage, have you?' she asked, glancing up Vicarage Lane.

It was Stephen who lowered his head and answered her inquisitive question. 'No, Mrs Prescott,' he said firmly. 'We haven't been to the Vicarage, we've been to look at Heron Cottage.'

'Oh!' She stared at them open-mouthed,

completely taken aback.

'It's up for sale, you know.' Stephen added, then with a wave of his hand he moved away from the kerb, leaving Lily Prescott standing in the middle of the pavement staring after them in astonishment.

'Oh, Stephen,' Helen gasped, 'you shouldn't have told her that! It'll be all over the village tomorrow!'

'What do you mean, tomorrow?' He gave a wicked chuckle. 'She won't wait that long—she'll tell them all tonight.' Then on a more serious note, he added, 'Nice of Oliver to go and see her, wasn't it?'

Helen nodded. It was typical of her father to do what he had, for, while he had been annoyed with Lily Prescott for not confiding in him sooner, and he'd made sure she'd known he was annoyed, he wouldn't allow her to worry one minute longer than was necessary.

As they turned into the drive at High Pines they noticed that several cars were already parked on the forecourt. Stephen grimaced. 'We really are late, aren't we?'

They hurried into the hall, intending to go straight to their rooms to change, but Mrs Parkes was waiting for them. She had a curious, tight-lipped expression on her face, but they had no time to speculate, for she said, 'Dr Meredith asked me to catch you when you came in. Would you please join him in the sitting-room?'

'Oh, dear, that sounds ominous,' said Helen. 'Perhaps we're going to be in trouble for being late.' She smiled at Mrs Parkes, but there was no smile in response as the older woman turned and walked back to the kitchen.

Helen pulled a face and, glancing over her shoulder at Stephen, was surprised to see that he was laughing. 'What are you laughing at?' she hissed as she turned the handle of the sitting-room door.

'The look on Lily Prescott's face when she thought something had been going on that she hadn't known about.'

They were still laughing as Helen pushed open the door—then they stopped and Helen's hand flew to her mouth.

Oliver was standing with his back to the fireplace, but sitting in an armchair, a glass of Oliver's best malt whisky in his hand and a quizzical expression on his handsome face, was Giles Patterson.

CHAPTER ELEVEN

Helen's heart missed a beat while Giles, cool and unruffled, rose to his feet, setting his glass down on the table beside him. His dark eyes narrowed slightly as he seemed to take in the situation while Helen, with Stephen behind her, stood rooted to the spot.

'Helen darling!' In two strides Giles was across the room and taking Helen by the shoulders he studied her face for a moment before drawing her towards him and kissing her cheek.

'Giles...I don't understand.' Helen, her senses reeling, at last found her voice. 'Whatever are you doing here?'

'I came to see you, of course.' He looked faintly bemused. 'Why else would I be here? Besides, I decided it was high time we talked.'

Helen stared at him. What in the world did he mean? Surely there was nothing left to say between them? Hadn't it all been said on that nightmarish evening when he'd told her he and his wife had decided to try and make a go of things? She looked wildly around, almost as if she expected Barbara to appear suddenly. But there was only Giles—Giles, looking every bit as handsome and assured as she remembered him in a beautifully cut designer suit and a black polo-necked shirt. As she desperately floundered to find something to say, Oliver cleared his throat.

'Helen, I have to go and start surgery,' he said hesitantly. The look on his face told Helen he was angry, and while his breeding would have demanded that he offer hospitality to Giles Patterson it was quite evident that he was reluctant to leave her alone to deal with a potentially explosive situation.

'Yes, Dad.' She made a supreme effort to pull herself together, but her voice came out as little more than a husky whisper. 'I'll join you in a few minutes.'

'You needn't worry about surgery this evening,' Oliver said as he moved towards the door.

'I wouldn't dream of missing it,' Helen replied. 'But perhaps you, Stephen, could explain to your first patient that I may be a few minutes late.' She turned as she spoke, but with a jolt she realised that the doorway was empty and Stephen had gone.

'It's all right, Helen, leave it to me.' Oliver paused at the door and looking back gave a curt nod. 'Good day, Patterson.' It was as near to a dismissal as he could allow it, as if he was telling Giles that he didn't expect to see him again.

As soon as he had gone, Helen rounded on Giles.

'Just why have you come here?' she demanded, only too aware that she was shaking with the shock of seeing him again.

'Why?' He opened his dark eyes wide in an expression of hurt innocence. 'I told you—to see you. And as I said, I felt we needed to talk.'

Helen took a deep breath, wishing her knees would stop knocking together. 'Giles, I think everything has been said between us.'

'Ah, but that's where you're wrong.' He smiled, a smile tinged with an air of triumph as if he knew something she didn't. 'There's plenty more to be said, believe me. However,' he glanced round at the sitting-room, 'I realise that this is neither the time nor the place. I've booked myself into a hotel in the West Wight and I've reserved a table for the two of us for dinner tonight.'

Helen almost gasped at his audacity, at his arrogant assumption that she would drop whatever she was doing and have dinner with him. 'I have a surgery to do,' she said firmly, then suddenly she caught the familiar scent of his expensive aftershave and a wave of nostalgia flooded over her. He, knowing her so well, must have seen the fleeting lowering of her defences, and he took his opportunity.

Stepping closer to her, he lightly touched her cheek with one slim brown hand, and she stiffened, drawing in her breath sharply.

'I've come a long way to see you, little one,' he murmured. 'Don't disappoint me...we really do need to talk, you know. Please, Helen?' Drawing his hand under her chin, he tightened his grip and lifted her face towards him.

He took her silence for assent. 'Go and do your surgery, if you must. I'll take myself off to the local pub and I'll be back for you at seven-thirty.'

She wanted to protest, to tell him that he

had no right to stampede back into her life and take over, but she seemed powerless to do so and could only stare helplessly as he gave her another peck on the cheek before sauntering to the door. Then with a wave of his hand he was gone.

Somehow Helen managed to pull herself together sufficiently to change into her uniform. Her duties that evening were mainly reception and clerical, and because Stephen stayed in his consulting-room she didn't see him. When the last patient had left and still he didn't appear she hurried upstairs to change, hesitating over what she should wear. Eventually she chose a plain black dress with only her gold earrings for adornment, as she didn't want to give Giles the impression that she had dressed up especially for him.

When she came downstairs it was nearly seven-thirty and she felt she ought to give her father some explanation as to what was happening. His surgery was empty, however, as was the sitting-room, so finally Helen went into the kitchen, where Mrs Parkes was sitting at the table solemnly drinking a cup of tea.

'Hello, Parky, do you know where my father is?'

Mrs Parkes nodded. 'Yes, he's gone to a meeting of the local Medical Council.'

'Oh, I'd quite forgotten that was tonight,' Helen said, then glanced sharply at the housekeeper. 'What's the matter, Parky, you don't look very happy?'

Mrs Parkes fidgeted in her seat, then setting her cup down in its saucer she looked up at Helen. 'I know it's none of my business, dear, but you don't have a mother to advise you, and I somehow feel responsible for you.'

Helen smiled. 'That's very kind of you, Parky, and I appreciate your concern, but I'm a big girl now and I'm quite capable of taking care of myself.' What she didn't add was that even if her mother had been alive she very much doubted whether she would be asking her advice over such an intensely personal issue.

'But why has he come here?' A worried frown creased the older woman's face. 'And after all this time.'

'I don't know why he's here, Parky.'

'Is he staying?'

'Apparently he's checked into a hotel and he's booked a table for me to have dinner with him.'

'Oh, dear, do you think that's wise?'

'Oh, Parky, you make him sound like some sort of pervert! You must remember that Mr Patterson is a highly respected registrar. I really don't know why he's come to see me, but I mean to find out. But please, don't worry about me.'

Mrs Parkes sniffed and standing up carried her cup and saucer to the sink. 'Well, I hope he's not here to try to persuade you to go back to him. I just feel he's not right for you. You've been so much happier just lately, and I was beginning to hope there was something between you and Dr Brett.'

'Do you know, Parky,' Helen laughed, 'you and Amanda should get together. You'd make a wonderful double act!'

The housekeeper frowned again, not understanding her remark, but Helen gave her no chance for further questions, for she continued by saying, 'Talking of Dr Brett, I was hoping for a word with him before I went out, but he doesn't seem to be around either.'

'He's out on a call. The community nurse rang at the end of surgery to say that Mr Osborne up at the Manor was deteriorating.'

'Oh, I see.' Helen knew that Mr

Osborne was terminally ill with cancer of the bronchus and that Stephen could be away for some time. She was half relieved at not having to face her father before she went out, but she had wanted to speak to Stephen, to explain to him why she was meeting Giles. But she had no further time for speculation, for at that moment the doorbell rang, and instinctively she knew it was Giles.

He was leaning on the open door of his black BMW, and he gave her his old heart-stopping smile as she stepped out of the front door.

'You look wonderful,' he said softly, taking in her simple black dress and her hair which tonight she had wound back into a chignon, knowing he preferred her to wear it loose. Moving aside, he offered his hand and helped her into the car, then took his own seat beside her.

As they moved out of the drive into the dark village street he said lightly, 'So how was evening surgery?'

Helen shrugged. 'Pretty unremarkable.'

'As I should imagine are most village surgeries.'

'You'd be surprised. We have our moments even in a rural community.'

'You do surprise me. In fact I still haven't got over the fact that you're actually working in general practice. I wouldn't have thought it your scene at all.'

'It's a job, Giles. And let's face it, I needed a job.'

'Agreed, but I would have imagined you going for something in the local hospital.' He threw her a sudden sharp glance. 'I take it you do actually have a local hospital?'

'Of course.' She was immediately on the defensive. 'And a very good one at that.'

'So could they not have found a position for you there? With your qualifications I'd have thought they'd have jumped at the chance.'

'I didn't apply.' Helen was conscious in the light from the dashboard of the surprised glance he threw her. 'I had intended applying, but circumstances proved to be different from what I had expected.'

'Tell me about it,' he said conversationally as they left the village and took the downs road to the West Wight.

Helen hesitated. She hadn't really intended giving Giles a run-down of her life since she had last seen him, but then he said,

'Did your decision have anything to do with your father?'

'Yes'

'Ah, I thought that might be it. Need a bit of help for a while, did he?'

'Yes, his list had grown out of all proportion and he'd been forced to take a partner. They decided a practice nurse was also required.'

'And you came along at just the right time. How convenient!'

Helen glanced sharply at him, for while there had been no obvious trace of sarcasm in his tone she couldn't be entirely sure. But she could only see his profile as he concentrated on the road ahead. For a moment she allowed herself to study him. The fine bone-structure, sleek dark hair and the high-bridged, slightly hooked nose. Once she could have gazed forever at that handsome profile.

'You won't be staying, of course,' he said suddenly, and it was a statement rather than a question.

'Why not?' Her reply was sharp.

'Why not? Oh, Helen, you can't be serious! What about your career? You can't be thinking of permanently burying yourself in this backwater!'

'I don't think of it as a backwater.' Her chin went up defiantly. 'Besides, it's my home.'

'That may well be, but from what I've seen of the place it appears to be about ten years behind the rest of the country.'

'That's its attraction,' Helen retorted.

They fell silent then and it became obvious that Giles wasn't going to discuss what he had come to tell her until later.

As they drew into the hotel forecourt she realised he had checked into just about the most prestigious hotel on the Island, and certainly the most expensive.

She stepped from the car and glanced up at the huge white façade and the blaze of lights, some which shone from behind the mullioned windows and others, hidden in the shrubbery, which suffused the gardens in a soft romantic glow.

'This is more the setting I associate with you, Helen,' murmured Giles. 'But my guess is there aren't too many places around here like this. You'd miss London if you stayed here. I know you would. You love the bright lights.'

'People are more important than bright lights, Giles,' she replied as they entered the hotel foyer. 'And I have friends here.'

'So soon?' The question was smooth.

'What do you mean?' She frowned up at him.

'You've made friends so soon?'

'Yes,' she admitted. 'I've made new friends and become reacquainted with some old ones.'

'And your father's partner?' His voice was soft now. 'You seem very friendly with him. Is he an old friend or a new one?'

Helen stiffened, then, as the hotel manager approached, greeting Giles by name and asking them to follow him to their table, she chose to ignore his pointed question. He had no right to ask such questions. He's lost any such rights when he'd ended their relationship, Helen told herself firmly as she took her seat in the elegant, Regency-style dining-room.

Throughout their meal Giles was the perfect escort, not once referring to her job or her friends again but talking mainly about life at St Luke's and bringing her up to date on all the gossip.

Helen found herself watching him closely and trying to examine her own response to him. During the past weeks she had imagined herself to be still in love with him and had thought that if she saw him again she would have difficulty in controlling her emotions. Now that her fears had become reality she found her reactions to be very different.

As he ate his meal she studied him carefully, his lean dark looks and impeccable clothes, but it wasn't until her eyes came to rest on his hands, those slim brown hands whose touch had once thrilled her so much that it struck her that she had unconsciously been comparing him with Stephen.

At the thought of Stephen she felt a quiver deep inside which seemed to spread throughout her body as she remembered their visit to Heron Cottage.

With a start she suddenly realised that Giles had been talking to her and because she'd been so lost in her thoughts she hadn't heard a word.

'I'm sorry, Giles. What were you saying?' she asked.

'You were miles away,' he said reproachfully. 'I was asking if you wanted to know why I'd come to see you.'

'Of course I do,' Helen replied crisply, trying to pull herself together and put Stephen out of her mind.

'I want you to come back to me.'

He said it quite casually and for a moment Helen thought she had misheard him, then with a noisy rattle she set her coffee-cup down in its saucer. 'What did you say?' She stared at him.

'I said I wanted you to come back to me.'

'Aren't you forgetting something, Giles?'

'What's that?' He raised his eyebrows, but a faint smile was playing around his finely shaped mouth.

'You do happen to have a wife.'

He shook his head. 'Not for much longer. Barbara and I are divorcing.'

Helen drew in her breath sharply. 'Why?' She looked at him suspiciously. He'd lied to her once; what was to stop him doing it again?

'Because, Helen my darling,' he leaned across the table and covered her hand with his, 'it just didn't work out.'

'I see. It didn't work out. So here you are, just like that, back to pick up where you left off with me.' She gave a short laugh, hardly able to believe what she was hearing. 'You really are unbelievable, Giles! You con me in the first place, omitting to tell me you're married, then you destroy my world by going back to your wife. Just as I'm starting to pick up the pieces you stroll back into my life and tell me that because it hasn't worked out as you expected you want me to go back to you!'

Helen's voice had risen, and Giles glanced round at their fellow diners, slightly embarrassed that they might have heard. 'Helen, please listen to me. You don't understand. Let me explain.'

'I can't see there's anything to explain...'

'There is...you see, it didn't work out between Barbara and myself because I couldn't get over you.'

'I don't want to listen...' Helen stopped in mid-sentence as she realised what he had said. 'What?' She stared at him, hardly able to believe she'd heard right.

'It's true, Helen. You must believe me. I just couldn't get you out of my mind, and in the end I had to tell her—Barbara, I mean—that I couldn't stay with her. Oh, Helen, you must admit that what we had was pretty special, wasn't it?'

'Yes, Giles, it was. But it's over now, there's no going back, and I just want to be left alone to get on with my life.'

'You don't mean that, Helen. You can't.' Giles leaned even further across the table, gazing intensely into her eyes.

'I'm sorry, Giles, but I do. I trusted you once and you lied to me, abused that trust. I could never trust you again.' Pushing her cup and saucer away, she stood up. 'Would you take me home now, please?'

'Sit down, Helen. I'm sure we can talk this through.' He spoke in a quiet controlled voice, but was obviously still conscious of the other occupants of the room.

'No, Giles. There's nothing more to be said. Now if you're not going to take me home I'll phone and ask my father or Stephen to come and fetch me.'

'Very well.' He stood up, tight-lipped and unsmiling, and they walked in silence from the hotel.

It wasn't until they were in the darkness of the car that he spoke again, and when he did there was a strange edge to his voice. 'It's him, isn't it? That new partner of your father's. He's the reason you won't come back to me.'

'I've given my reason for not coming back to you, Giles. I'm sorry, but you'll just have to accept it.'

'I refuse to accept it, Helen. I felt so sure of you. Why don't you give it a try and see how it works out? Come to the flat and spend Christmas with me.' As he spoke he slid his arm along the back of her seat and stroked the back of her neck.

She shivered. 'You still have the flat, then?'

'Yes,' he replied eagerly.

'So where's Barbara?'

'When she left she went to live with her sister. I assure you she really has gone this time.'

'So she left you, Giles?' Her voice was suddenly cold.

'Well, not exactly...'

'You led me to believe you'd left her because you were still in love with me when in actual fact, she probably left you because she couldn't take any more. That's about the truth of it, isn't it Giles?' As she felt the anger well up inside her she jerked herself way from his hand.

He stared at her for a moment, then he shrugged and, leaning forward, switched on the ignition.

They drove back to Dyer's Mead in silence, and just as they turned past the church Giles glanced at Helen. 'No chance you'll change your mind?'

She sighed, more with exasperation than

regret. 'No, Giles. I'm sorry, but no chance.'

'Ah, well, you can't blame me for trying. After all, it really was good while it lasted, wasn't it?'

She smiled in the darkness. 'Yes, it was.'

As they pulled into High Pines Giles said, 'Tell me one thing. Is it him? The new partner, I mean?'

'It might be,' she replied, unwilling to commit herself, then as the house came into view she sat up straight in alarm.

A police car, its blue light flashing, was parked at the entrance. As Giles brought his car to a halt Stephen appeared in the doorway with a uniformed officer.

Helen scrambled from the car and leaving the door open behind her ran across to Stephen. 'What is it, Stephen?' she asked anxiously.

'A domestic dispute up on the new estate,' he answered, his gaze flickering for a moment across to Giles. 'Brian Arnold, Maureen's husband, is threatening suicide and has barricaded himself in the house with their young son. I'm going to try and talk him out.'

'I'll come with you,' replied Helen without a moment's hesitation. 'I know Maureen and the children. I may be able to help.' She had begun to walk towards Stephen's car when he nodded towards Giles, who was still sitting in his BMW.

'Don't you think you should tell your friend?' he said curtly. 'I'll turn the car round.'

'Oh, yes.' Helen started guiltily. She had quite forgotten Giles. Turning, she walked rapidly back to his car, but this time she approached the driver's side.

Giles wound down the window. 'What's going on?'

'A crisis with a patient. I'm going to see if I can help.'

'Helen, I'll be going back in the morning.'

'Yes, I thought you might. Goodbye Giles.'

He stared at her for a long moment, his expression a mixture of irritation and incredulity, then with a shrug he raised his hand and gave a rueful smile.

Helen turned again and ran towards Stephen, who was waiting for her with his car engine running.

CHAPTER TWELVE

Stephen said very little on the drive up to the new estate on Skinner's Fields, but Helen wasn't sure whether this was because of Giles or because of what might be awaiting him at the Arnold household.

They followed the police car, its blue light flashing, and when they turned into Sorrell Close, in spite of the lateness of the hour, they could see little groups of people on the pavement.

Sorrell Close was a cul-de-sac of attractive semi-detached houses that had been thoughtfully designed to blend in with the environment. But tonight this was the last thing on Helen's mind, especially since the policeman had told Stephen that Brian Arnold had a shotgun in the house with him.

As they drew up behind two police cars she threw Stephen an anxious glance. 'Is he capable of carrying out his threat?'

'I wouldn't like to say. But he's visited me recently and I've been treating him for depression,' Stephen replied.

'Did you know he'd been made redundant from the factory?' asked Helen as he switched off the engine.

Stephen looked at her in surprise. 'No, he didn't tell me that. I asked him if everything was all right at work and he said it was. But how did you know?'

'Maureen told me when she came for her smear.'

'I wish I'd known. I wonder why Brian didn't tell me.' Stephen frowned as he peered up at the darkened bedroom windows of number twenty-six.

'I got the impression that they're very proud,' said Helen quietly. 'When I told Maureen they could get financial help she was quite indignant and called it charity.'

'Well, I've got some idea how to approach him now.' He paused and wound down his window as a police officer approached the car. 'What's happening, Officer?'

'Dr Brett, is it?' The policeman crouched down alongside the car. 'He's up in one of the bedrooms. We think the boy's upstairs as well. According to his mother he wasn't feeling well and went to bed early.'

'Poor little lad,' said Stephen. 'Have you

had any communication with Mr Arnold recently?'

The police officer shook his head. 'Not really. There was the initial incident with his wife when she tried to get into the house with her daughter. Then he barricaded himself inside, shouting that no one was going to take his home away. Then when two of my men attempted to enter the premises he threatened to kill himself.'

'Did he say how he intended to do it?'

'Yes, he said he had his shotgun. Apparently he belongs to the local gun club.'

'Did he at any time threaten his son?'

'Not as far as I know, Dr Brett. Now, what do you intend to do, and how can we help?'

'I'm going to try to persuade him to come out,' Stephen replied. 'I know him and I'm sure I can do it. I'd like you to radio the hospital and speak to the duty psychiatrist, explain what's happening and tell him I'm going to try for a voluntary admission. If I'm not successful, we may have to call him out along with a social worker.'

'Shall I go and talk to Maureen, Stephen?' asked Helen.

'Yes, that's a good idea. She may tell you a bit more. Where is Mrs Arnold, Officer?'

'She's over there with a neighbour, number thirty-three,' said the policeman, pointing across the road.

'Right, let's get started then,' said Stephen, but as he went to get out of the car, Helen touched his arm and he looked back at her enquiringly.

'Stephen,' she said as her eyes briefly met his, 'be careful. Please.'

He nodded, but his expression was grim, and with a feeling of dread in her heart she watched him walk up to the group of policemen outside the house, then, accompanied by two of them, he disappeared up the pathway.

Maureen Arnold was sitting huddled over her friend's kitchen table, her thin hands curled round a mug of coffee. She looked up quickly as Helen, followed by a WPC, came into the room. Her frightened glance darted from one to the other.

'What is it? What's happened?' Her voice was hoarse, barely more than a whisper.

'It's all right, Maureen. Don't worry, nothing's happened,' said Helen, then added, 'I've just come to talk to you for a bit. Dr Brett's gone over to your house—he's going to try and talk to Brian.'

'I don't think he'll listen—he wouldn't even listen to me. It was as if he didn't even know who I was—me, his own wife! God, it was awful!' Her voice broke and she wiped her eyes with her hands.

'Where's Beverley?' Helen glanced round, but there was no sign of the little girl.

It was June, Maureen's neighbour, who answered. 'I've put her to bed with Nicola, my daughter. They're great friends and I thought it would be for the best.'

'Quite right,' replied Helen. 'It's best to keep things as normal as possible where children are concerned.'

'But what about Scott?' A great gulping sob suddenly came from Maureen. 'Oh, I'm so worried about Scott!' She twisted her hands in anguish and Helen leaned across the table and gripped them tightly.

'Maureen, listen to me. Scott will be all right—I'm sure of it. You told the policeman he's gone to bed, didn't you?'

'Yes,' Maureen nodded. 'He wasn't feeling well...' Her eyes filled with tears again.

'Well, there's a very good chance he's

asleep and doesn't know anything about all this.'

'But Brian's not himself—he doesn't know what he's saying...what he's doing.'

'Maureen,' June slipped an arm round her friend's shoulders, 'Brian would never harm Scott. Why, as far as he's concerned the sun shines out of those kids.'

'I know...but he's changed so much.'

'Can you tell me about it?' asked Helen gently.

Maureen swallowed, trying to steady her voice. 'Well, he's been depressed for some time now.'

'Do you know why?'

'Not really. He went to see Dr Brett about it and he asked him that, but he didn't know why.'

'But can you remember when it started?'

Maureen frowned. 'Well, I suppose it goes back to before we moved here.'

'Did anything unusual happen about that time?' asked Helen.

Maureen hesitated, her frown deepening. 'Not that I can remember...apart from his mother dying.'

'And don't you think the death of his mother could have been a reason for his depression?' Helen asked the question gently as she sensed there might have been friction between Maureen and her mother-in-law.

Maureen stared down into her mug. 'Well, we all have to face up to things like that, don't we?' she said at last.

'But did he have time to grieve for her?' Helen persisted.

'No, I suppose not.' Maureen gave a slight shrug, then shook her head and her expression softened. 'It was so sudden, you see. She was killed in a road accident and soon after that we moved here, and what with buying the house, and Brian starting his new job, there wasn't time for anything. But,' she glanced up at Helen from under her sandy eyelashes, 'I suppose you could be right. He was always very close to his mother.' She said it in a resigned sort of way, and Helen knew her earlier assumption had been correct.

'Did Brian's depression get worse?'

'Yes, I suppose it did when he was made redundant.' Maureen glanced up. 'You remember I told you? He just couldn't accept it when it happened. The final straw, you might say.'

'But did anything in particular trigger this incident tonight?'

Maureen was silent for a moment as if battling with some inner emotion, then she looked up, first at Helen, then to June as if for support, then back to Helen. 'It could have been a telly programme we saw about a family who couldn't pay their mortgage and in the end their home was repossessed...and the kids were taken into care. I think...I think it must have played on his mind. We had a row about money this morning, then tonight I went to collect Beverley from her Brownie party, and when I got back he wouldn't let us in.'

As she was speaking there came the sound of footsteps and voices from outside, and the WPC stepped forward and opened the back door. Stephen was standing on the threshold, and as Maureen looked up and saw him her hand flew to her mouth in alarm.

'It's all right, Maureen,' he hastened to reassure her. 'I've been trying to talk to Brian, but he won't answer me. He's going to need some help when we do eventually persuade him to come out—you do understand that, don't you?'

She nodded and her mouth trembled again. 'You mean a mental hospital.' She said it fearfully, not as a question but in a resigned sort of way.

'It will be for the best. They'll be able to give Brian the help he needs, but what I would like is for him to agree to go in as a voluntary patient. I'm going to go back and have another try, but I wondered if you have any ideas of how I might get through to him.'

Maureen helplessly shook her head, then gently Helen touched her arm. 'Maureen, tell Dr Brett about Brian's mother,' she said.

Stephen listened carefully while Maureen related the story and when she had finished he straightened up. 'Thank you, Maureen, that's just what we needed. I'm sure I'll be able to get somewhere now.' He gave Helen a small, grateful smile, then he was gone again, leaving the women to wait.

It was a very long wait, stretching far into the cold December night. June made endless cups of tea, not only for Maureen and Helen but for Stephen and the police officers on duty.

Twice more during the night Stephen appeared, once to reassure Maureen that he was almost certain that her son was asleep and the second time to say that it looked very much as if he was going to have to call the psychiatrist and have Brian committed to hospital. He looked cold, tired and defeated this time, and Helen's heart ached for him as she watched him sip a mug of hot tea.

'Would you like to phone from here?' asked June with a worried glance at Maureen, who seemed to have slipped into a state of silent shock.

Still Stephen hesitated, and Helen knew he was worried that if they had to use force to get Brian Arnold out, harm might come not only to him but to Scott, who would certainly wake up and become involved.

Then suddenly Stephen seemed to reach a decision and stood up, draining his mug. 'No,' he said, 'I'm going to have one last try. It'll be better for everyone concerned if he goes voluntarily.' Purposefully he strode from the house while Helen, still fearful for his safety but filled with admiration, watched him go.

And it was then that it came to her, quite suddenly and without the shadow of a doubt, that he was the man she wanted, the man she loved. Giles Patterson might be quite exceptional at surgery, but he had neither the compassion nor the strength of character of Stephen Brett.

Barely an hour later a policeman came to tell them that at last Brian Arnold was communicating with Stephen through an open window. Up until that point, although Stephen had been certain Brian was listening to him, he had not uttered one word in response.

But it was to be a further hour before the waiting women heard voices outside and the sound of a car's ignition being switched on. Minutes later the same policeman who had been keeping them informed of what was happening appeared, and this time, looking at Maureen as he spoke, he said, 'It's all right, Mrs Arnold. It's all over.'

For a moment Helen saw terror flicker in Maureen's eyes, then the policeman added hastily, 'No one has been hurt. Your husband talked to the doctor and he persuaded him to throw the shotgun out of the window. Shortly afterwards he came out himself and agreed to go directly to the hospital in a police car.'

'And Scott?' breathed Maureen, her eyes enormous in her white face.

The policeman smiled. 'Apparently the little lad slept through it all. There's a WPC with him now, and he's still asleep.'

'Oh, thank God!' Maureen slumped down in her chair just as Stephen, fatigue etched into every line of his face, appeared and asked to use the telephone to warn the hospital of Brian Arnold's imminent arrival.

It was nearly five in the morning before Helen and Stephen left Sorrell Close and drove through the deserted village to High Pines. There had been a heavy white frost and the hedges and rooftops glistened in the light from the car's headlights.

At the corner of Vicarage Lane they passed the milkman on his early morning round. Helen glanced up the lane and found it difficult to believe that it had only been the previous afternoon that they had visited Heron Cottage. So much had happened since that it seemed as if it had been days earlier.

She was still dressed in the black dress she had worn for dinner with Giles, and in spite of her fur jacket she shivered in the chill of the winter's morning.

High Pines was in darkness, and when they quietly let themselves in, even the dogs could only manage to lift their heads in greeting before burrowing down into the warmth of their baskets again.

'It hardly seems worth going to bed,' said Stephen as he followed Helen into the kitchen.

'I was thinking the same thing—I'm dog-tired, but I don't think I could sleep. Shall I make us some tea?'

'I've drunk enough tea to sink a battleship.' He sighed. 'How about some coffee for a change?'

'Coffee it is, then, and some toast.' Helen busied herself with filling the kettle and putting some slices of bread into the toaster. 'Will the Arnolds be all right?' she asked Stephen as he spooned instant coffee into a couple of mugs.

'I hope so. We can't do any more for the moment except give support to Maureen and the kids.'

'Will there be any charges against Brian?'

'I shouldn't think so. No one was harmed.'

'Thanks to you.' Helen glanced at him over her shoulder and was struck again by how tired he looked and unusually dishevelled, with a dark growth of stubble on his chin.

'I don't think I could have done it unless you'd told me about his mother—that was the key factor, you know.' He watched her as she buttered the thick slices of toast. 'As soon as I persuaded him to talk about her death the floodgates opened. After that it was only a matter of time before he came out.'

Helen looked thoughtful. 'I gathered from Maureen that he hadn't had any time to grieve for his mother.'

'That may be so, but I hadn't known it was a case of delayed grief. He hadn't even mentioned his mother's death when he came to me with all the classic symptoms of depression. If only people would give us all the factors, how much easier our job would be.'

'From what Maureen said,' said Helen slowly, 'I got the impression that natural emotions like grief may be somewhat suppressed in the Arnold family. I doubt they even considered it as a symptom, more like something that happens to everyone, something to be coped with, just like the fact that they'd consider it charity asking for help with paying their bills.'

'They really are going to need some help in one way and another.' Stephen yawned and passed a hand across his face. 'I'll get on to the social services about them later.' He looked across the table as Helen set down his plate of toast and it seemed as if for the first time he became aware of the way she was dressed.

'Thank you for coming with me,' he said stiffly, then frowned as he added, 'I guess it cut short your night out.'

Helen shrugged as she bit into her toast. 'Not really, it wasn't that sort of an evening.'

He stared at her keenly. 'But what about Patterson? I wouldn't imagine he'll be too happy about you disappearing so abruptly.'

'That we shall never know,' Helen replied casually.

'What do you mean?' Suddenly Stephen seemed to have lost the defeated look he had had and appeared wide awake.

'He's going back to London this morning.'

'And you, Helen?' he asked quietly. 'Will you be following him?'

'Me?' Again she tried to adopt a nonchalant tone. 'Oh, no, I shall be staying here.'

'And what's made you reach that decision?' His tone was quiet.

Feeling the colour tinge her cheeks, Helen looked down at the tablecloth, suddenly unable to look Stephen in the eye. 'I've come to the conclusion,' she said softly, 'that the role of a GP's wife in a village practice is much more my scene that running a surgical ward and living the high life in town.'

He stared at her as if he could hardly believe what he was hearing. 'But when you went out with Patterson last night...I thought...'

'You shouldn't jump to conclusions.' She glanced sharply at him.

As hope flared in Stephen's eyes he leaned across the table and taking Helen's hands he gripped them tightly, compelling her to look into his eyes. 'If that's the case, why did you go out with him? I'm afraid I automatically assumed the worst.'

'I had to go, Stephen. I find it difficult to explain, but there was something about my relationship with Giles that was haunting me, something that was preventing me from loving you. Only by seeing him again, talking to him, could I sort myself out.'

'And did it work?' His grip tightened and she knew he held his breath as he waited for her reply.

'Yes, it did.' She smiled, and as she read the expression in his eyes her heart seemed to turn over. 'You may find this hard to believe, but I ended up almost wondering what I'd seen in him in the first place. They say love is blind, and I think I believe that now. Giles Patterson may have a brilliant career ahead of him, but he certainly isn't the man for me. Stephen, do you understand what I'm trying to say?'

He nodded. 'I know only too well what you mean.' She raised her eyebrows in surprise and he continued. 'You remember I told you there was once someone very special in my life?'

Helen nodded and bit her lip as an unmistakable pang of jealousy shot through her.

'Well, I really was smitten with her. Her name was Zoe; she was a nurse, and I met her in Africa. She wasn't interested in a serious relationship, and I came back to this country thinking I'd never get over her.'

He paused, reflecting for a moment, then as Helen squeezed his hand, he went on, 'I saw her once more, about a year later, and I too ended up wondering what all the fuss had been about. So, my

243

love, I know exactly what you mean.' As he spoke he stood up and moved round the table, then, their breakfast forgotten, he pulled her into his arms.

For a long moment she gave herself up to the ecstasy of being in his arms, then his lips claimed hers in a kiss so full of passion that it told her all she needed to know about his intentions.

At last he drew away and looking down into her eyes he murmured, 'Well, that settles what I need to do first this morning.'

'And what's that?' she asked dreamily, her eyes searching his face and coming to rest on his finely shaped mouth.

'A phone call to the estate agents to make an offer for Heron Cottage—that is if you think you could bear to spend the rest of your life there with me, away from the bright lights of the city.'

A teasing note had crept into his tone again, and Helen smiled and lifting her hand gently traced a line down his face, allowing her fingers to move lightly across the stubble on his chin, then coming to rest on his lips. 'Oh, I dare say I could force myself to come to terms with it,' she whispered.

Stephen looked at her intently, his mood changing. 'I'm serious, Helen. Life is quiet here, and you've been away for a long time. Do you really think you could adapt again?'

'I've been back long enough to know that this is the type of life I want. My family and friends are here, and as for village life being quiet, I'm afraid I'm going to disagree with you there. There's been more going on here in the last few weeks than happened in six months in London.'

'So your answer is yes?' he asked.

'Oh, Stephen, of course—but—' suddenly she paused and her hand flew to her mouth '—aren't you forgetting something?'

He raised his eyebrows and she continued, 'I'm not certain that I should marry you.' She smiled as she saw his frown. 'After all, wasn't it you who said members of the same family shouldn't work in the same practice? I don't want to give up my job, so not only would we have father and daughter working together but husband and wife as well.' A mischievous note had crept into her voice, and at that moment they heard Oliver's foot on the stairs as he came down to make his early morning tea.

Stephen gave her another quick hug. 'There is an exception to every rule, my love. Now, who's going to tell your father? You or me?'

'Shall we tell him together?' Helen asked happily as the kitchen door opened.